BOOKS BY CHLOE RIGGS

Soulmates are Overrated

Sense of Love Series:

Falling for the Sound of You

Reviving From the Touch of You

REVIVING

FROM THE

TOUCH

OF YOU

ISBN: 978-1-968366-06-3

REVIVING FROM THE TOUCH OF YOU

CHLOE RIGGS

BLOOMING NARRATIVES
blooming-narratives.com

First paperback edition June 2025

Cover design by Chloe Riggs
ISBN: 978-1-968366-06-3 (paperback)
ISBN: 978-1-968366-09-4 (hardback)
ISBN: 978-1-968366-08-7 (ebook)

For the warriors looking for the person to clean your
weapons and hold you in between battles.

REVIVING FROM THE TOUCH OF YOU

PROLOGUE

Camila's blood turned cold at the sight through the crevice of the bedroom door. Ben, the man she thought would be her forever, laid on top of another woman. To make matters worse, instead of screaming the name of an unknown woman—someone Camila could digest a little easier—he screamed the name Elizabeth.

No.

She shook her head and swallowed the lump in her throat.

He said his engagement to Elizabeth wasn't real. It was all publicity. He said—

Her foot bumped into an end table as she backed up from the scene, causing a jagged ceramic vase to fall. Quickly, Camila caught it to prevent it from crashing against the floor.

He couldn't know she was here. *She* couldn't know.

It didn't matter if Ben was the asshole or cheater in this scenario. His fame and popularity would save him and destroy Camila before she even had a chance to get a foot in the door of the movie industry.

Camila set the vase back on the stand carefully, blinking the well of tears in her eyes away, and booked it to the door. She grabbed her shoes and carried them against her chest as she ran away.

Only when she reached the stairwell, deciding the elevator was too cramped, did she realize blood poured down her leg from a long cut on her thigh. It pooled between her toes and coated her blue painted toenails in a new shade of a violent purple.

She sank to the ground with her back against the cold wall as the dam broke loose.

Being a stunt double, cuts and injuries never bothered her. They hurt and sometimes even made her bedridden for a little while, but she always fought through the pain.

In that moment, even just the air grazing against the wound made the spot pulse and the drips of red caused her stomach to sour.

Eventually, she'd have to call her brother to come pick her up and he would demand she go to the hospital. But for now, she battled the sobs she heaved as the organ in her chest throbbed worse than the cut.

> **Insouciant**: showing a casual lack of concern.
>
> **Indifferent**: having no particular interest; neither good nor bad; neutral.

It could be from how white the patient's knuckles were as they grip the arm of the chair—or because Jason had been skimming the 'I' section of the dictionary earlier, but these two words swam in his mind as he studied the woman sitting on the hospital bed in the center of the room with a blank expression on her face.

There was a gash on her leg, the skin around it red and raw as Dr. Palmer swept a needle in and out to stitch the wound.

The other man in the room, someone with the same jet-black hair and tan skin as the patient in the chair, held her shoulder gently. He whispered comforting words to her, despite keeping his attention averted from the cut.

The woman, however, stared intently at the wound with the emptiest look in her eyes like she expected the cut to disappear at any moment, but also wasn't surprised to find the injury either.

An instinct to stand beside her, offer her his hand to squeeze—the only form of communication he knew how to produce properly—coursed through Jason.

Yet Jason continued to stand off to the side, observing the situation like the studious resident he was.

Residents aren't supposed to step in. Not when their teacher was the same man that could terminate their career with a flick of his wrist.

He only had a few months left before moving into his fellowship role in the ER. A little while longer and then he will be the one helping patients.

But the sight of her lack of pain, void of all emotion, and how tightly she still gripped the arm of the chair…

It caused a weird palpitation in Jason's chest.

Jason's attention fell back on the woman with short black hair who bit her lip so hard he wouldn't be surprised if it started to bleed too.

It took everything in him to not stand beside her and squeeze "it's okay" with her hand in his.

CHAPTER ONE

CAMILA

A YEAR AND A HALF LATER

I am going to murder, strangle, maybe swing an axe at, Paxton Marie Martinez. The bloodier and more painful the better.

"Come visit," he said.

"It'll help get your mind off Ben," he insisted.

"You spent money on plane tickets, anyway," he noted.

Except the plane tickets I originally paid for was a two-week vacation to a sunny island with Margaritas and Ben lying on the beach beside me. A trip to finally be together in public and not tucked in the shadows hiding. A trip that was supposed to occur over a year ago.

Not a month-long trip to a region without taxis or guides or even a street sign to direct where I'm supposed to go. A deserted location that apparently has an abundance of snakes if the one slithering and eyeing me is anything to go by.

Paxton never showed to pick me up from the airport. He hasn't answered any of my calls or texts.

Meaning, I'm on my own.

It started out fine. I managed to convince someone to give me a ride on their way to their own destination, but we eventually reached a fork in the road. They went right and let me out to walk left. According to them, who knows this land a heck of a lot better than me and my unavailable GPS, I would only need to walk for a few miles to reach where Paxton is.

Hiking in a dry dirt area with a large suitcase and worn tennis shoes is not what I had planned for this afternoon. Especially after a long flight unable to sleep because of a screaming child a few rows back and a man who couldn't decide between a bag of pretzels or a bag of nuts beside me.

I walked around the curve of the trail only to stop when the sound of hissing caught my ear. Funnily enough, a snake slithered out of the bushes and into my path. It's long and coffee-bean colored. Entirely too intimidating for my taste.

Now I'm stuck between a potential threat and turning around to walk back to the airport and hop on the next flight. If Paxton really wanted me here, he would have made sure to pick me up.

"You sure you want to spend the next month with your annoying brother?" The memory of Lily's question to me as I pulled my suitcase from the back of her parents' car comes back to my mind.

"He's been begging me," I said, which is partly the truth.

She knows I'm visiting Paxton at the refuge he's working at in another country, but she doesn't know the real reason as to why he wouldn't take no for an answer.

"All I'm saying is, he doesn't seem like the type to know how to navigate tying his shoes, let alone survive in another country."

I rolled my eyes. Another thing about Lily and Paxton: they despise one another.

"Lily, I have to go."

She gave me a hug, and I tried my best to reciprocate without seeming awkward or uncomfortable. Then Lily offered to take my place for me instead. I declined on the grounds of wanting to see Paxton, but also not wanting to get a call that one of them is in jail.

Now, as I meet the threatening eyes of the snake swaying in front of me, I wish I could travel back in time and have Lily fly out here instead.

"Easy," I whisper to the animal as if it has ears, and hold a steadying hand up.

I've dealt with snakes before on set. It's part of the job as a stunt double. I get the scenes no one else wants, but there has always been a handler on set in case things go wrong with the animal.

Out here in the wild terrain of Sub-Saharan Africa, there is no one trained to handle slithering threats.

If I'm lucky, something I haven't experienced in the past few months, it will let me pass.

"I'm just going to go that way and…you can keep doing your *thing*?"

Its tongue pokes out as it stands a little taller, slithering closer.

Do snakes smell fear?

Shit.

I knew better than to listen to my idiot older brother and here I am.

Taking a step closer, I say a little prayer.

If this thing bites me, Paxton will be ground to a pulp before he has a chance to so much as utter, "I'm sorry."

The clumped dirt and gravel crunch under my shoes as I move slowly. The snake stays rooted to its spot, only moving in an intimidating dance side to side.

When I'm within two feet of it, the sound of tires crunching on the road draw my attention away and behind me.

Right as a cruiser fills my line of sight and I attempt to raise my arms up to signal, something digs into my shin. "Mother fu—"

I bend over in pain as the snake slithers away, victorious, and I'm left with two fang marks in my skin. Expletives fall from my mouth faster than I realize what I'm saying.

"Fucking useless, cowardly, slimy, beast."

My eyes squint from the pounding ache in my head and the pulsing pain in my leg as I stare at the spot the attacker slithered into.

"I don't think that boulder has ears." A male voice floats to me.

I snap my head up to find a man with short dark, windblown hair and a pair of clear rimmed glasses perched on the tip of his nose. He's dressed in a tan scrub, nearly blending into our surroundings.

I'd say he looks as if someone released him into the wild from a hospital, but he appears entirely too confident out here with his arms crossed over his chest.

"Do you always annoy victims?" I hiss through my teeth, tightly gripping the wound on my leg.

His eyebrows push together as he studies me. "Victim?" He glances around us, searching for something.

It's then that I realize I am alone in the wilderness with a bite the size of an apple in my leg and a strange, irritating man who could overpower me in an instant.

Could this day get any better?

"I don't..."

Reaching the conclusion that if he wants to kill me, he will anyway, I point to the shrub where the snake slithered away. "There was a snake."

As if realizing I'm hunched in pain and not on the ground for my own personal enjoyment, his gaze falls to the spot my fingers are digging into.

Then, muttering something under his breath, he moves closer and kneels in front of me. He reaches a hand out to the wound, but I stop him by swatting his hand away. There's a weird buzz from his skin to mine in that half a second, but I blame it on the heat and chunk of skin missing on my leg.

"What are you doing?" I demand.

He stays frozen, but there's obvious impatience lingering his expression. "I can't help you if I don't see it."

"I don't need your help." God, why am I turning down his help when I'm practically in tears from how bad this stings?

"Really?" He stands, tucks his hands in the pockets of his shirt, and stares down at me. "Then I guess you're able to walk."

Because I'm more stubborn than a mule apparently, I release a shaky breath, let go of my leg, and slowly rise from the ground.

Unfortunately for me, my foot twists in the process and I fall back down on my butt, hard.

"Can I look now?" The man asks, still watching me.

The second I find Paxton, he's dead meat.

CHAPTER TWO

JASON

Annoyed doesn't even begin to describe the emotion coursing through my veins right now. Who denies help when they've been bitten by a snake and are clearly stranded?

The woman with the dark brown hair falling out of the small ponytail she tied it in as she sits hunched in pain on the ground, apparently.

"Go for a drive," Dr. Robins demanded.

According to her, I'm not pleasant to be around when I only have an hour or two of sleep energizing me, which apparently makes the rest of the team nervous.

"Find something to perk you up."

Yeah, not sure a stubborn woman on the side of the road is the key to that, but here I am. I couldn't very well leave her stranded when I watched her go from standing tall and waving her arms around, to shrinking to the ground.

I pulled the car over without an ounce of hesitation and climbed out to help her. She must not have noticed me because the second I got within earshot, I heard a string of unintelligible curses leave her mouth as she stared at one of the boulders or small shrubs to her left.

By the looks of her, she's new to the area and probably fresh off the plane if the suitcase is anything to go by. The worn sneakers on her feet aren't built for this type of terrain and her layers and layers of clothing are too much for the heat around us.

Sweat drips down her face and the edges of her short, dark hair. The strands of her hair are matted and sticking to her skin. At least, the pieces that have fallen from the half-broken hair clip on the side of her head.

"Can I look now?" I ask, impatiently.

She glares up at me from her spot, her hands still tightly gripping around the wound above her ankle.

I doubt the bite was poisonous. She doesn't seem to be having trouble breathing or on the verge of passing out. But I have no way of confirming that if I can't check it for myself.

She doesn't say yes or no, just releases her grip and leans back slightly.

Hesitantly, I crouch down in front of her again. I reach a tentative hand towards the spot, noting the slight prick of hair on her skin, and curse when I see the bite.

There are two prominent holes in her leg across from one single dot a few inches away in the center. A triangle of fang marks and all three are swelling.

"How bad is the pain?"

"Do you mean on a scale of one to ten?" the sarcasm oozes from her.

I try my best to not scowl, but my mouth fails me. "Humor me."

Through gritted teeth, "I don't know. A manageable five?"

"Are you dizzy or lightheaded at all?"

"A little but that could be because I haven't eaten for a few hours."

A few—

This girl is going to be her own death if the bite isn't venomous.

"What about a headache?"

"I'm starting to get one with all of the questions."

I fix her with a pointed look and try my best to keep my grip on her leg gentle. "Do you want my help or not?"

I'm a doctor through and through and it is not just my job, but my passion to help people. Including stubborn people who don't know kindness if it slapped them in the face. But that doesn't mean there isn't any small part inside of me hoping she will say no, stand up, and walk away.

If this were all one big nightmare, I wouldn't be disappointed.

She sighs, "A small one. Yeah."

"What did the snake look like?" I've only been in this territory for a little over a month now, fulfilling the three-month timeframe I am to volunteer with the medical team here, but I've been learning.

I've taken heed to all of the warnings from the members of my team who know more about wildlife than me, as well as the ones who have visited this area before.

I'm from New York City and have never been to any countries outside of my own before. Sub-Saharan Africa happens to be bare, dry, and full of dangerous threats if you aren't careful.

It's mostly a safari with rainforests spread out. There is very little rain and a heck of a lot of sun. It's more intense than the city and far from what I'm used to.

During the weeks leading to my departure, I studied meticulously every plant, animal, or other natural things native to this culture. I prepared. And if I'm right, that bite could be one of two. One being more dangerous than the other.

My only hope is she doesn't say—

"It was brown."

The urge to roll my eyes is strong. "Any chance you've got a better description? Nearly every snake around here is brown or has a spot or two of brown."

"I'm sorry I didn't do a sketch of it before it attacked me," she says sarcastically, moving her hands to her bent knees and defeating the little space between us.

"Fine. A brown snake. Could be one of two."

"What two?" Her voice starts to rise in concern. "What does that mean?"

I study the bite once more, carefully running my finger along the wounded skin, which elicits a soft inhale from her. Based on her symptoms and the lack of bleeding, it's probably just a Brown House Snake.

"Stay put," I tell her before standing and walking back to the car.

"Wha—you can't just leave me here!" she yells at my back.

I don't bother responding and instead busy myself with finding the equipment I need.

"Hey! What the hell is going on? Am I fine or not? You can't just—"

She stops talking when she sees me pull out a radio and speak into it. "Dr. Robins."

Static clips in and out of the device. "Copy, copy, copy. Have you found your smile yet?"

I'm sure the radios weren't meant for us to discuss personal matters, but I ignore it and calmly request, "I'm going to be back at the refuge in about thirty minutes. Can you prepare a stretcher and…" I check over my shoulder at the woman who stared daggers at me only moments before. Now, she looks *scared*.

Lowering my voice and turning back around, I mumble into the device, "Brown Snake antivenom."

Whispering was useless because the reply is loud and clear. "Did you get bit? Jason, you know better than to wander when you aren't in a group."

"I'm fine. It's for someone else. Just get the stuff ready, please."

She gives me a curt yes and the conversation ends. Carrying the plastic box we keep in the vehicle; I make my way back to the woman on the ground.

"Wha-what's antivenom?" Her voice is wobbly, but I can tell she's trying to sound confident and unafraid.

Here she is scared shitless and I'm being the biggest ass.

I crouch in front of her again and reach for her leg. She swats my hand away for the second time, and the contact between our fingers sends a weird sensation through my body. Her next demand quickly makes that feeling dissipate, though.

"Don't touch me until you tell me what the hell the bite is. Is it…poisonous? Am I…?"

"No."

I don't let her finish that thought, nor do I correct her on the fact that snakes are venomous, not poisonous. If patients think death is close or even remotely possible, they are more likely to faint and the last thing I need is for her to become a deadweight.

"There's some minor venom in the bite, but it's nothing that can't be treated."

Honestly, it might not even be venomous at all and she's likely fine, but I'd rather not take the risk. It's also a bit of a plus to get under her skin the same way she's getting under mine.

I reach for her ankle again and this time she lets me. Gently, I stretch her foot towards me, removing her shoe in the process.

"Is that," she starts as I slide her foot from the sneaker, but the shoe is already off and discarded beside us before she can finish her sentence with, "Necessary."

Normally, I would walk the person through what I have to do. Sometimes it calms people to be in the know of the situation. In this instance, I think she's the type who'd rather be kept in the dark.

So, I don't utter a word as I do my best to fashion a makeshift split and position her ankle. For some unknown reason, her skin is burning hot under my touch. Or maybe it's me that is so warm, but something about my fingers on her leg is making me sweat.

It must be the sun beating against my back and the irritation still lingering inside me at her stubbornness.

When it's in place and the best it's going to get, I hook her shoe with my finger, grab her suitcase, and toss both in the back of the car.

"What are you doing?"

"I assumed you didn't want to leave your stuff stranded on the side of the road," I grumble.

She eyes me from her spot on the ground. "Where are you taking me?"

I reach a hand out to her in hopes of helping her up, but she just stares at it. Through gritted teeth, "To a refuge where I work. They have the equipment and treatment you need."

"That's who you were calling on the walkie talkie?"

"Yeah."

She reaches her hand up to mine, then slowly raises it back down. "How do I know you're telling the truth and not trying to lure me somewhere?"

Intolerable: more than can be put up with.

This is the word swimming in my mind as I stare down at her. Filtering words and definitions through my head is a habit I picked up after years of reading and rereading the dictionary as a hobby.

"You don't," I say. "But unless you want to wait for the next vehicle, which won't be for at least another few hours, I'm your only hope. You're just going to have to trust me."

She chews on her bottom lip, weighing her options. Honestly, with how she's been acting towards my kindness, I could care less about helping her. Except, turning around and driving away sends an unsettling feeling to my gut.

"You've always been a giver," Jasmine told me countless times.

She always knew about my dream to become a doctor and start my own practice. She supported me in every way and was the backbone I needed when I wanted to start my career anywhere but at the hospital Mother happens to be the director of.

I don't want to be tied to Mother's name and image. I want to be known by *my* expertise.

When I thought about pursuing a different path because of that, Jasmine kicked me back onto the road and made Graham stand guard, ensuring I never veered from my dream.

Although Graham, being the best of best friends he is, never had a problem with pushing me.

Take now for example: despite being an ocean away, his nagging voice is in the back of my head, demanding I stay and help this woman.

Shaking the thoughts away, I bend down beside her and soften my expression. "Let me help you up so we can get you help. Then, once you're healed, I'll drive you home."

There's no way she lives around here just by the looks of her alone, but that's not the point. I just need to get her in the c—

Her hand claps onto my shoulder as a silent agreeance. Not wanting to argue or change her mind, I adjust her grip on me, ignoring the weird sensations shooting from her skin to mine, and lift her up and book it to the site.

CHAPTER THREE

CAMILA

Doc—that's what I've decided to call the man who found me on the side of the road in pain from a snake bite, but the scrubs he's wearing are only a small part of the reason why—pulls to a stop in front of a small, but wide building.

It's one of three similar sizes in the area, plus a few tents and cabins. The place is spaced out between structures, but it can probably be driven in one clean circle. The refuge is definitely sketchy, but it's not as suspicious as I expected. I've been trying my best to stay alert and study our surroundings the whole ride here in case I need to escape later. That proved harder than necessary, though, with the throbbing in my shin and dizziness setting in.

If there weren't so many bumps on the drive jostling me, I might have fallen asleep.

When Doc rounds the vehicle to my side and opens the door, my jaw sets at the item outside the car.

"I'm *not* getting on that."

He smirks, knowing I have no choice but to. "If you want treatment and to keep your leg, you will."

Keep my leg?

I assumed there was poison in my bloodstream from the strange cast around my ankle and the demands he gave through the walkie talkie, but losing a leg? *That* was never mentioned.

Fuming, I take the hand he offers, confused at the flutter of energy coursing through my veins at his gentle touch, and make my way onto the stretcher. It's not a classic stretcher from the hospitals in the city. It looks more like one you buy or use simply because it can get a person from one place to the next.

It wobbles and creaks beneath me, but no one—including the woman I now see standing to the side of it—seems worried.

The woman starts to wheel me inside, muttering things to the man who brought me here.

"I told you to go out and have *fun*. Not get a girl bitten."

"I did," he tells her. I can't see either of them since they are behind me, but I feel the annoyance in both of their tones. "She got bit all on her own."

That seems to be the end of it because they stay quiet all up until they reach a room with a clear curtain hanging from ceiling. A dull, blue light illuminates the space, making it eerie and sterile inside.

The woman stands to the left of me, pulling something from a shelf, while Doc stays on my right, studying me. Like I'm some kind of specimen.

"Um," I start, but it comes out scratchy. I clear my throat and try again. "Not to seem ungrateful, but who exactly are you two?"

"You didn't even introduce yourself, Jason?" The woman chastises him.

He rolls his eyes. "There wasn't much time in between all of the bi—" He stops himself, seeming to think better of it. Rubbing at the back of his neck, he turns his attention to me. "I'm Jason."

"And you are…what?"

I tell myself the interrogation and talking is to keep myself distracted and busy and awake while the woman produces a needle much larger than necessary.

I don't usually shy away from those things. I love horror movies, and, unlike Paxton and Lily, blood and needles don't bother me. But with the gloomy atmosphere and having no one I recognize in the room, I'm suddenly dizzier than before.

The people occupying the room with me start to blur, along with the furniture around us. I try to blink everything into focus, but it proves futile.

Passing out is the least rational thing to do right now amidst strangers in an unknown location with no service.

Maybe it's the bite and I'll wake up to all of this being a dream.

Or maybe I'm delusional and am asleep on the plane.

Yeah, that seems like a much more reasonable response.

My eyes feel heavy, and I notice Doc's lips moving, but I don't hear any sound coming from him. Instead, the noise of crickets chirping like the ones in my parents' backyard growing up fills my mind.

I open my mouth to call out to them and ask what this fuzzy feeling in my limbs is, but my tongue is too heavy and dry for any words to roll off of it.

The pair doesn't seem to notice my efforts, though. At least, from what I can make out of their blurry forms.

Then, the woman and Doc disappear completely, and the rest of the world goes black.

"Are you sure that works?" a familiar, but fuzzy voice floats to my ears.

I slowly blink my eyes open, but my vision is blurred and there's a bright light shining in front of me. Attempting to sit up, a pounding ache in my head makes itself present, but I fight the wince.

Why do I feel like I drank ten bottles of beer in one night?

"Like I said the first ten times, yes. It works." A different man grumbles.

"Then why is she still—Camelot?"

It's a nickname I recognize even in this fog. Paxton has called me it since we were little and exposed to Arthur and Merlin. I became obsessed and would challenge the stuffed animals and Ottis, our family poodle, to duels with the foam sword we bought at a fair.

I ran around the house shouting, "Save Camelot!"

So, Paxton started calling me Camelot and it just happened to stick.

After a few more blinks, my vision clears enough for me to take in the sight around me. I'm on a stretcher in between two clear curtains hung from the ceiling. An IV is connected to my arm and sunlight is streaming in through a window across from me.

The sterile room isn't what catches my attention, though. Doc is standing in the corner with his back to me as he rummages on some metal tray.

A hand grips my shoulder, and I turn to my left to find the reason I'm even lying here in the first place.

"You're awake!" Paxton exclaims before crushing me in a giant hug. My lungs nearly combust under the pressure.

"Get," I choke out as I pat his back, hard. "Off. Me."

He pulls away and stares down at me with a sheepish expression. "Right. Sorry. I'm just so glad you're alright."

"Alright?" The word comes out loud and scratchy, irritating my head even more. "I was fucking attacked, Paxton."

A chuckle comes from the corner. Doc's shoulders shake a little as he shakes his head.

"Is something funny to you?"

He twists to face me, not even bothering to mask the amusement in his eyes. "No." He crosses his arms and raises a brow. "Except you weren't attacked."

"Yeah? What do you call *this*, then?" I point to the bite on my leg, noticing it's now wrapped in gauze.

How long was I asleep?

"You got hurt, but you weren't *attacked*. Attacked implies the snake intended to kill you or used violent force. He simply nibbled your skin."

Nibbled my—

I should have stayed asleep.

"Sorry, I didn't realize you were Webster's Dictionary."

Doc's head tilts as he studies me with a curious gleam in his expression. His eyes have a darker tint to them inside this box and his hair looks as if his fingers have gone through it once or twice.

Apparently, I'm not the only disheveled one here. It sends a thrill through me to know I get under his skin as much as he does me.

"I'm sorry," Paxton interrupts. "Do you two know each other?"

Neither Doc, nor me, look to my brother when we say, "No," at the exact same time.

"Cool." Pax blows out a breath. "Well, if she's cleared to go, I'll take her."

"She's cleared," Doc informs him, turning back to the tray he was messing with a moment before. "Just keep her ankle elevated for a few days and make sure she eats."

With that, he leaves the room. Paxton calls "thanks" out to his retreating form.

When Doc is out of the space and his annoying personality has floated out with him, I turn all of my frustration to my brother.

"Hey," he holds his hands up in front of him. "What's with the death glare?"

I cross my arms, ignoring the tense ache in my muscles as I do so. "Oh, I don't know, Pax. Maybe I'm just a little upset because you forced me to come here, ditched me at the airport, and are the reason I'm lying in a fucking hospital bed."

"You're upset."

"You—"

God, I could kill him. About a thousand ways filter through my mind and I can make every single one look like an accident. Not that I care about being arrested right about now.

Trying to keep my temper in check, I ask, "How did you even find me anyway?"

"I was visiting Ginger—Dr. Robins, the woman who treated you—when she mentioned a particularly stubborn woman Jay found on the side of the road."

He adjusts the camera hanging from his shoulder and wraps one arm around my shoulder to help me off the bed.

"What's the odds the person who found is one of the doctors leading the medical team here?"

This makes me pause with my feet hanging off the edge of the bed and Paxton's hands gripping mine tightly. "This is the refuge you work at?"

Please say no. Please say no. Please say no.

There's no way on Earth I am going to spend an entire month in close quarters with Doc. Being around such an insufferable, entitled human being is not the vacation Paxton promised me.

"Yeah. It's pretty amazing, isn't it?" His words are full of excitement.

Paxton loves photography and people. Being a humanitarian photographer is the job created for him. I can feel the energy beaming off him about it in the same way I could hear over the phone the past year.

He's annoying and thinks he knows better, but I missed him. Seeing him in person after a year and a half apart, it's all finally settling in.

My chest swells with warmth as I realize I'm finally somewhere he can protect me. He couldn't save me from Ben. He wasn't home to prevent all of the depressive spirals I experienced after.

He happened to be around the day I found out and is the one who took me to the hospital to get the cut on my thigh stitched up, but then he left. Off to his next adventure for his job and leaving me alone.

Living alone in a studio apartment the size of a shoebox and an hour or so from our parents' house has never been a problem for me before.

Lily visits at random hours and it's much easier to find Paxton than it is to get rid of him.

After I walked in on Ben sleeping with Elizabeth and now having a scar on my thigh to constantly remind me of the event, I hate being alone.

It's when all of the doubt decides to leave the shadows of my mind and creep into the memories of Ben and me.

How long did it go on? I asked myself constantly.

Did it just happen that day or have I always been the other woman?

The answer to that question hurt the most. I had always thought Ben would propose to me after the advertisement for the movie faded out and their contract for the fake engagement ended. Turns out, there was never any contract, and I can be much more easily manipulated than I thought.

The younger version of me would go around with a sword and claim I could save the kingdom or the castle. I didn't need anyone to save me.

When Paxton got on the plane the day after everything, though, I felt the most helpless I have ever felt in my lifetime.

I was just a broken girl who wished her older brother would beat up the man who ripped my heart into shreds.

But he's here now and the last thing I'm going to do is let that doctor ruin it.

I start to shift on the hospital bed again and Paxton helps me off the stretcher. "Please tell me you at least have running water."

"Running in what sense?"

"I'm going to kill you."

He laughs, and despite how annoyed I feign to be, I'm at ease.

CHAPTER FOUR

JASON

I dip my cupped hands in the well of water, splashing the liquid onto my face. It's the only source of cold in all of this heat. One of the problems in this region is the lack of technology and resources.

Not only are the family's experiencing famine, which leads to more complications like disease, but there's a shortage of water and electricity.

The lack of electricity and internet is not something I'm concerned about, though. It means less phone calls from Graham about things as unimportant as "streaming Netflix with him."

"Why would I do that?" I asked him when he first proposed it to me before coming here.

"Because Piper goes out with Hazel and I get lonely in this big place all by myself." The crunch of the popcorn in his mouth was audible.

We share an apartment that has two bedrooms, one bathroom, a kitchen and a living room. It's pretty small for two guys our size, but it works. Although, it doesn't allow me enough space to escape said roommate.

"Watch it by yourself," I said.

"Why would I do that when I have such an amazing friend as you?" It was a comment layered with sarcasm.

Luckily, the lack of internet and access to electric saved me from having to come up with an endless list of excuses. Graham knows I'm not the sitting down and watching a movie type, anyway, so it's clear he only tried to pull my chain.

I dish out a lot of crap to him, but he's a good friend and important to me. Will he ever hear me say that aloud, though?

He has a better chance of convincing Piper to go to one of the galas Mother throws.

Another reason I appreciate the escape from the online world: Mother can't watch over me like a hawk from this far. Although, it wouldn't surprise me if she paid one of the nurses that came with to keep an eye on me and report back.

She's worried I'll back out of what I promised before I left. I can't say I blame her for how long it took me to finally agree, but this has been a long time coming. If I planned on ending it, I wouldn't have even bothered with suggesting it.

"How's Paxton's sister?" Dr. Robins asks as she pats a hand on my back.

I scrub my face with the bottom of my shirt, exposing some of my skin in the process. "He took her back to his tent the last I checked."

"Good. I'm sure she's dying to get back on her feet after coming here on such rugged terms."

Rugged doesn't even begin to describe it. From how dramatic she made it seem, I'd say the correct descriptors are disastrous, life-altering, and a few other words that would compute the world ending.

Why Paxton would invite his sister who so clearly hates the outdoors is beyond me.

Him and I met when I arrived a few months ago. I pulled luggage out of the back of the cruiser when an arm hung over my shoulder and someone shouted, "You're here," in my ear.

Quickly, Paxton realized he had the wrong person and apologized. He only removed his arm after I unapologetically shrugged out of it.

We don't talk much, but that has everything to do with my lack of tolerance for people than it does his personality.

Honestly, he's about one of the only people here I can stand. The others being the ones who actually reside here. The natives don't annoy me like my team does.

"Paxton thinks it will be good for her," Robins' gaze falls on a spot behind me and I turn to see the siblings crossing the terrain and heading towards the dining hall.

Camila, that's the name Paxton gave me for her, is limping slightly as she leans her weight on Paxton. He must have mumbled something to her, because she starts to chuckle and throw her head back.

Then she shoves him to the ground and laughs harder. I expect Paxton to stand and be pissed—it's how I would be if she shoved *me* to the ground—but he simply laughs from his spot on the ground and says something unintelligible to her.

"Don't even think about it," Dr. Robins warns from beside me.

I tilt my head to find her shaking hers. "Think about what?"

"He brought her here to keep her away from relationship problems. Not find her a new one."

At this, I release a small laugh. "Trust me, he doesn't have to worry about me." Never has a sentence been truer.

"Hey," Sam, one of the nurses who accompanied us on this volunteering expenditure, comes up beside me as I stand a few feet from the fire and the circle of people around it.

I tip my beer bottle towards her in acknowledgement.

"It's a nice night out, isn't it?" She stares up at the star-filled sky above us, casually whipping her head back and forth to sway her long, auburn hair behind her.

I never understood why girls used their hair as weapons of seduction. What about strands from someone's head do men find so attractive?

The only thing that catches my attention about a woman's hair is if it's been washed or not, which is probably not what they want someone like me to notice.

"Mhmm," I hum back.

There's no doubt in my mind Sam likes me. In the hospital, she'd convince other nurses to swap patients with her, so she had more time with me. I never said anything about it because, while her intentions are misplaced, she does her job, and she does it well.

It didn't surprise me in the least when I saw her name on the list of people coming here. Nor did I bat an eye when she slid into the seat next to me on the plane.

I did lose a few bucks on the plane ride, though, because I had to pay one of the other nurses to swap seats with me when her head continued to fall on my shoulder.

Women have attracted me before, but never enough for me to lose all common sense or indulge the idea of pursuing them. Mother snubbed that idea in the butt before it had time to fester.

She always pushes me closer and closer to Jasmine and further from any other women. Jasmine is smart, beautiful, and highly successful with her own perfume company.

We grew up together and our parents set up play dates every week, which later turned into *subtle* dates as we got older.

It happened so often, our fellow classmates and friends assumed we were dating, despite how often we corrected them. The few women I found interest in, refused to flirt back because of Jasmine, and the ones who did flirt with me, only did so to get under Jasmine's skin.

The same happened for her. Every guy in the school was too scared of what would happen if they hit on Jasmine.

So, we eventually got used to being pinned together and just went with it.

No matter how hard we tried to fall for each other or become attracted to the person our parents wanted us to, we couldn't seem to get past that friend threshold.

Well, not until recently, that is.

"It is a little chilly, though," Sam shivers beside me, running her hands up and down her arms and eyeing the jacket I have on.

She's only wearing a spaghetti strap tank top and I'm sure it's on purpose.

It stays hot and humid in the daylight, but it can reach chilly temperatures when the sun sets. Ironic how much this place relies on the sun.

"I think there's extra hoodies in the storage wing," I note, keeping my attention on the people around the fire.

My gaze wandered from person to person, watching some laugh, one person belt out in song, and a few just watch the others with a smile.

No matter how many times I forced my attention away, though, it continued to find the woman with short black hair whose skin is still a burning memory on my fingertips.

I barely touched her and yet, it's like she implanted herself on me. There's still a strange tingle in my veins when she's near, like my body can sense someone annoying. The same woman who doesn't know "thank you" if it slapped her in the face.

Scoffing, I take a sip of my beer.

"Right," Sam croaks from beside me. "I forgot."

Camila adjusts her leg in its position propped up on a makeshift stool Paxton produced for her. I may have exaggerated when I said to keep it elevated for a few days, but it lit a fire inside me to see the irritation bubbling within her when I did.

Everyone is dancing and carrying on around her, including her brother, and she's smiling too, but even from this distance and the little light the fire creates, I can tell it doesn't reach her eyes.

It's the same way she acted on the side of the road. Yeah, she yelled and cursed and sent a few death glares my way, but none of them seemed to match the pain I imagine the snake bite gave her. She almost seemed numb to it.

She's putting on a front.

Dr. Robins' words from earlier come back to me as I watch Camila from my spot. *He's trying to keep her away from relationships.*

Why? What happened that led her to come here and sit so indifferently around a fire with a bunch of strangers?

"I…" Sam starts again, but I don't turn to look at her. "I think I'm going to go join the rest of the group."

Silently, I nod.

"I'll save you a seat in case you want to join too." She lingers for a moment, waiting for me to say something, but I don't.

Instead, I keep my attention focused on the newcomer with question after question filling my mind. Camila must sense my presence because she turns her gaze my way. The second our eyes meet, something stirs to life inside me, but I stay perfectly still. Not one muscle of mine moves as I study her.

When her lips pull down in a frown and one of her brows quirk up, finally showing some type of emotion, I smirk.

Tracking her emotions is not one of the ways I plan to spend my last month here. Noticing a different woman is not something someone like me should be doing.

Yet, a tally mark is suddenly struck in my mind as Camila scowls at me.

Chapter Five

CAMILA

I shift in the cot, listening to it squeak beneath me. Paxton must be passed out because he doesn't grumble at me about the noise like he did the last few times I rolled over.

Luckily, he didn't have a roommate to share this tent with, so he grabbed an extra cot from the storage building, dusted the cobwebs off of it, and set up a few feet from his bed for me to sleep on.

"It's comfier than a hotel," he advertised after covering it with a thin sheet and an even thinner blanket. Then he plopped down and bounced once or twice, only proving the frail item could hold his weight.

I'm not spoiled by any means so sleeping on a cot with a breeze winding through the opening of the tent does not bother me. What does bother me is Paxton's snoring.

He groaned and complained about me keeping him up, but here he is now. Passed out and probably shaking the canopy around us with how loud he is. No wonder he doesn't have any roommates.

I roll onto my back, wincing at the ache in my leg from the movement, and stare at the ceiling. I try to picture sheep jumping over a fence and count each one, in hopes it will tire me enough to drown out the rest of the world.

I haven't slept well since Ben. He rarely ever stayed the night, and I was never allowed to stay in his bed in fear someone would catch us. That's what it's like dating a celebrity who is supposedly dating someone else in public.

Elizabeth Rose Stevens. The lead actress in the rom com they filmed together. She was the Allie to his Noah, except the names of their roles were Felicia and Hudson. Not as catchy.

To promote the movie and encourage viewers, their publicists decided to push them together in public. "Romance bloomed in the most unlikely of places," was the headline for weeks.

Not sure if falling in love with a costar you acted in love with was unlikely, but I'm not a marketer or publicist.

From halfway through shooting to a half a year after, the two were pictured as the best couple of the century. Women wanted to be her if only to hang on Ben's arm and men wanted to be him to have Elizabeth on theirs.

I happened to be the stunt double for one of the lesser roles in the film. I noticed Ben once or twice—I'd have to be blind not to—but I never acted on it. It didn't make sense for someone of my caliber to be with someone like him. Especially since he was taken. At least, that's what I thought until one night when the crew all went out for drinks.

Ben and I eyed each other from our diagonal spots at the table. When he caught me staring, he'd wink, and one corner of his mouth would tilt in the hottest smirk.

After my fourth drink of the night, I excused myself from the table. I was on my way to the restroom, and he followed me, spinning me around and pinning me to the wall to kiss me, apparently.

Too lost in surprise and dizzy from the alcohol swirling inside me, I didn't stop it from happening. Not until after his hand found its way under my shirt. His cold touch against my hot skin seemed to be enough to eliminate the trance.

"What are you doing?" I shoved Ben's chest to pull his mouth from mine.

Ben's mouth quirked with a grin as he leaned back, but he didn't move or give me more than a few inches of space. "I believe it's called kissing."

I blushed like a schoolgirl. Then scolded myself internally for it. "I got that part, Ben. But what about…"

I didn't know how to get the words out or say what really plagued my mind. Back then, I wasn't in on the publicity stunt. No one was. To everyone but Ben, Elizabeth, and their agents, they were madly in love.

"Aren't you and Elizabeth dating?"

The idea of becoming the other woman, especially with a man who caught my attention and made my heart flutter, sent nausea coursing through me.

He grinned wider. Butterflies began dancing in my chest. "No. It's just for publicity."

Looking back, I should have asked more questions. I should have pushed him away. The wicked smile on his lips and the taunting touches he left on my skin should have been enough warning to shove him away and turn on my heel. But I didn't.

I liked Ben. During shoots, I'd watch him on set and become enamored with his acting. I'd watch his arm loop around Elizabeth and the green monster would find its way in my stomach.

Sometimes, I thought he noticed me too. We would occasionally meet each other's eyes across the room and it felt flirtatious, like a secret. But I ignored it and told myself it was all in my head. He was supposed to be with Elizabeth after all.

Except, Ben kissed *me* in the secluded hallway of some bar and grill. Not her.

So, I let my body take over. I let his hands roam and his lips creep along my jaw. I even did the same to him by snaking my fingers along his abs and sucking at his bottom lip.

I let my heart control my actions then and I did it again for the two and half years we dated. Never again will my heart be allowed to take the reins.

Sighing, I pull the sheet off me, swatting the imaginary sheep away, and stand.

If I can't sleep, I might as well stretch out my leg a little bit.

The bite above my ankle still stings occasionally and I'm told I'm not allowed to travel far. Supposed to keep my foot elevated. But the swelling went down, and I feel fine.

I'm fine.

When I step outside of the tent and into the night, I'm taken aback by the lack of lighting. It's different being in the wilderness than in a busy city like New York. Here, the only lighting is from the glow of the moon.

I decide to take a lap around the camp in hopes it will help to clear my mind. It's already two in the morning and lying there isn't getting me anywhere.

My sneakers—I forgot to pack a pair of boots, but Lily managed to sneak in a few dresses—tread against the clumped dirt with a soft crunch.

I agreed to go on this trip in hopes Paxton is right and it will help me get out of this funk. I'm over Ben. I've been over him since the day I caught him in bed with the woman he claimed there was nothing between.

According to Paxton, I'm still pinning for the relationship I never had. But he's also the same person who claims mustard on pizza is delicious.

Yeah, a wise one he is.

"Can't sleep?"

I nearly jump out of my skin at the sudden question and look up from the ground to see none other than Doc leaning against a building and staring at his hands as he fiddles and thumbs his left ring finger.

"Do you make it a habitat to sneak up on people?" I hold a hand over my heart, willing it to calm down.

He stays in the same position with his arms crossed, but he tilts his head at me. It's hard to make out his expression in the darkness, but I imagine him with that knowing smirk. Or a roll of his eyes.

"I was here first."

"Real mature." He's right, but I don't like it.

He stays quiet, but continues to observe me like I'm some specimen he wants to poke and prod. Even silent he's insufferable.

"Do you like lurking in the dark?" I'm a jerk, I know I am, but I can't help it. I've been playing defense for almost a year now and it's not an easy position to switch out of.

"Couldn't sleep either," his words are soft, and it somehow releases the tension in my shoulders. Suddenly, he pushes off the wall, shoves his hands in the pockets of his hoodie, and starts to pass me. "I'll go so you can be alone."

Be alone? He's leaving the spot he clearly seemed at peace in just so I can be alone.

The same man that is annoying by existence.

Yeah, I don't think so. My luck, there's some snake or raccoon or bear lurking nearby and he knows it.

I turn in plans of heading back to the tent. No way am I getting attacked again, and alone in the dark, nonetheless.

Doc peers at me over his shoulder and asks, "Why are you following me?"

"Paxton's tent is this way."

"But you were heading that way until you saw me."

I cross my arms, Paxton's jacket bunching around me. Mine is covered in dirt from my fall this morning so my dear old brother granted me with one of his. "Maybe you bored me enough for me to fall asleep."

"Glad to be of service," he grumbles.

We fall into step with one another, letting only the nature around us fill the silence. Our arms occasionally brush against each other, and even through the sweatshirt, there's a weird tingle coursing from him to me.

Strangely, I don't feel the urge to put distance between us. His touch and my body's reaction to it makes me want to step closer.

Shaking the idea away before it has time to fester, I shift to my left. The last thing I need is another man getting in my head. Especially one as arrogant as Doc.

"So, Doc—"

"That's not my name."

I nearly groan aloud like a kid who's been told no. "It's called a nickname."

"I didn't ask for one."

"That's the point. You don't ask for nicknames; they're given to you. Wouldn't it be a little narcissistic to give yourself a nickname?"

He stops us outside of a row of tents and tilts his head at me. "Does that mean I can give you one?"

Something weird settles in my gut. Despite the warning in my head, I nod. "Sure."

"How about Snake?"

My hands fall to my side as I look at him incredulously.

"Or Venom?" He smirks, tapping a finger on his chin. "Maybe Bane?"

"That's not how nicknames work." I don't mention that I have no idea what the word 'bane' means, but it's probably an insult.

"Ah, ah," he waggles a finger at me. "Didn't someone say you don't decide your own nickname?"

My teeth grind together in irritation. I would have had a better time standing in the dark by myself and risk being open to any unforeseen dangers than following him.

Doc changes the subject by mentioning, "Thought you said you weren't following me."

"I told you, I—"

"Heading back to the tent. Yeah. But isn't Paxton in the row we passed?" He points behind me and that's when I realize we're in a different row. The row I didn't venture in earlier because it's for the medical team on site.

I open my mouth to retort, create some type of comeback or excuse as to why I got distracted enough to keep walking, but he turns around before I have a chance.

"Good night, Bell."

Bell? He's either comparing me to the instrument or the Disney princess. I'm not a fan of either.

CHAPTER SIX

CAMILA

"Are you planning on stewing on the cot all day?" Paxton asks me from the entrance of the tent as he slings the camera over his shoulder and reaches for another bag.

"I'm not stewing." Technically, I'm lounging.

After my run in with Doc last night, I managed to get about an hour or two of quality sleep. Although, holding Paxton's nose to wake him up and tell him to stop snoring probably helped a little more than the walk.

Either way, my entire body is groggy and not ready to face the full blast of sunlight yet.

"You came here for a reason, Camelot."

"To relax. I'm relaxing." I snuggle further into the thin blankets, despite the sweat beginning to lick at my skin.

"You're such a liar. I've never seen you sit still a day in your life."

True, but not the point. If I go out there, I might run into *people*. People aren't someone I want to see right now. Not after embarrassing myself last night and being called "Bell." I still haven't figured that code out yet.

Is he saying he's the beast? Yes, Doc is grouchy and intimidating by just the look of him. I've only been here for a day now and I can already tell he likes to keep to himself.

But in no way am I his beauty in this entire scenario.

And the instrument? He couldn't possibly think I resemble an object that pings and is used to alert people.

All of his snarky comments float back to me and that thought seems to be even more plausible.

I tried to make nice and be friendly and he gave me a name to essentially call me annoying.

Asshole.

"Come on." Paxton tosses a ball cap with the Batman logo on it at me, not caring that the lip of it smacks me in the cheek. "I'm not letting you sit in here all day. You have to at least come out and eat."

My stomach growls in agreement. I haven't eaten anything since last night and even then, it was only a granola bar.

If I wanted something more, either the cooks would have to reopen the kitchen and scrounge up a meal for just me, or I'd have to make something on my own out of the packs of food available. Beans or rice made my stomach gurgle.

So, I said I wasn't hungry and grabbed a granola bar from Paxton's stash instead. Probably another reason I feel dead right now.

"Fine," I groan as I sit up and tuck my head in the hat. "But I'm still mad at you for ditching me."

"I'm sorry, alright?"

He leads me out of the tent and towards the dining hall. It's an old religious building turned into a mass dining room.

"I forgot to reserve one of the vehicles and they were all gone before I got up. Won't happen again."

Yeah, but only because I will never trust him about taking a trip again. I should have known better with how horrible he was with being on time growing up. He showed up late to school so many times the teachers believed his lie that he thought school started at eight, not seven.

Our parents were never strict on that kind of thing—just as long as we graduated—so they never felt the need to intervene in Paxton's horrible manners as a student.

"Yeah," I mumble, "when pigs fly."

His camera brushes my arm as we walk. "You know, you've been quite the grump the whole time you've been here."

"It's only been twenty-four hours."

"My point."

He's right. I have been unusually testy since I got off the plane, but I have a valid reason.

Not only did I land in a country I've never been, get stranded on the side of the road, bit by a poisonous snake, and meet the most annoying man known to exist, but I also have nothing beckoning me back home.

My contract ended for the last show I did and there's currently no upcoming projects interested in me, or so Kyra has said. So, I don't have any work obligations tying me there.

My parents are there, but they are living their best lives in early retirement now that Paxton and I are out of the house.

I'd like to think Lily is missing me, but she doesn't *need* me. In between her housekeeping jobs, writing, and travelling around town, I'm not sure she even has the time for me.

The only place I feel I sort of belong is here with Paxton and even it is a small reassurance.

So, yes, I've been a bit of a grump, but for good reason.

There's not even a dojo around here like there is in the city for me to occupy my time and battle the demons in my mind.

It's just…dirt.

"Good morning, Paxy," a woman coos from outside the medical building as we pass.

I turn to see it's the same woman from yesterday who argued with Doc before I passed out. She's older than I remember, evident by the few wrinkles around her eyes and the spots of gray at the tips of her hair.

"Morning, Ginger," he plants a kiss on her cheek.

My brother has never had an issue with affection. Our parents used to joke the storks delivered him from Europe because of how easygoing he is with touch.

I used to be that way too. Not as affectionate as him, but not one to shy away from the ones I love.

It was all I craved a year ago. So much so that I didn't bat an eye when Ben entered my apartment and greeted me with a kiss. There wasn't so much as a word uttered between us before our clothes fell to the floor and moans filled the silence.

Then, he left for meetings and appointments.

I never blamed him. He's an actor and he has responsibilities that come before us. I'm sure it'd be the same if I were the one in his position.

So I didn't force him to stay longer, nor did I insist he skip work. Instead, I absorbed every endorphin his touch gave me and savored them until the next time we saw each other.

"There's a package for you in the back," Ginger tells him. Then, she turns to me with a smile. "I see you're feeling better."

"I am," I agree. "Thank you for your help, by the way. I didn't get to say it yesterday."

She waves me off. "Don't worry about it. It was mostly Young who helped you."

Young. That must be Doc's last name. Not that it matters though.

I nod, not knowing what else to say, as Paxton starts to sort through the pile of packages at Ginger's feet. "What did you order?"

"Remember those cookies Mom would buy after church?"

My mouth waters at the memory. "The ones with cinnamon and baked apples?"

He grins as he picks up a box with his name printed on the label.

"Please tell me that's what's inside that box."

"Depends. Are you going to forgive me if I do?"

Shrugging, "I'll consider it."

He laughs softly and tosses the small parcel to me. I rip it open without a second of hesitation. The tape isn't as tough as I anticipated, though, and my arm ends up swinging high as I pull with too much force. My hand connects with something hard, my knuckles bruising with the impact, as an exclamation fills the space behind me.

I turn my head to find Doc standing behind me with his hand over his nose.

"Sorry," I say sheepishly.

Paxton roars beside me with laughter and Gringer joins in. Doc, on the other hand, sends me a death glare.

Yeah, he's not going to let this go.

"Pocket knives exist," he grumbles as he slowly moves his fingers from his nose and inspects them for blood.

He's not bleeding, but the tip of his nose is turning a soft shade of red. If his skin wasn't as pale as it is, it wouldn't even be noticeable.

I place my hands on my hips; the small box still clutched in one of my hands. "Didn't need it."

Doc maneuvers around me and to one of the seats at a foldable table at the edge of the entrance to the building. He sits and continues to inspect his nose with his fingers, occasionally wiggling his nose in the process.

His black hair is combed and styled on the top of his head, a feat I imagine will become more and more impossible as the humidity increases during the day. There are no glasses perched on his nose like yesterday, but he's in another set of tan scrubs.

I wonder if that's the color of the hospital he works for. Ginger is dressed in a casual t-shirt and a pair of cargo pants, however. Maybe it's some odd mannerism or habit of his. He certainly seems like the type to be particular about his clothing or hair.

"Don't even think about it," Paxton elbows my side, and I realize I was staring. *And* smiling.

What Pax doesn't know is that I smiled out of victory. Doc could use a few beautify marks on his chiseled face. No one ever looks as put together as he does right now and I almost pray the humidity hits sooner.

Laughing the ridiculous notion away and covering up the fact that my gaze latched on to the cute wiggle of

Doc's nose, I push at Paxton's chest and move past him with the box in my hands.

If there's one thing Paxton doesn't have to worry about it's me getting involved with Doc. No matter how cute his nose wiggles are.

CHAPTER SEVEN

JASON

"Jason," Robins calls out from behind me as I wrap a band around the boy's arm who stands in front of me.

Part of our mission here is to provide as much free medical care to the residents as we can. This includes vaccines for all of the children the parents' give us permission for. Some parents aren't as willing, but I can't say I blame them.

If I were dealing with a government that isn't able to fund areas like this and prevent starvation and sickness, I would be weary of outsiders too.

"Yeah," I call back to Ginger without looking over my shoulder.

I've done this rodeo enough to insert the needle in my sleep, but the last thing I want is to risk hurting the boy. Especially when his arms are more bone than fat and muscle.

I make a mental note to check the food supply later. If there's a break in the schedule, maybe I can dish some snacks out to the kids.

When I have children of my own, they will have access to more food than they will know what to do with. The last thing a child should have to worry about is where their next meal is coming from. Jasmine has always agreed with me on this, but she also worries about her children's relationship with food.

A kid should enjoy their food. Not stress about calories or what it's made of or use it to eat their feelings.

After growing up in houses like that, we have learned what not to do.

"Where's your radio?" She demands.

Because of her lack of urgency, I'm assuming there's no one in danger so I don't know why she's asking about the radio.

I finish the vaccine, bandaging the spot and handing the boy one of the cookies I stole from the lounge before the shift, and turn to her.

"I left it in my coat pocket," I peel the gloves off my hands and point to the open door of the building.

Stevens and Jude were radioing to each other back and forth during storage inventory as if they were some spies on a mission. The nonstop static and conversation made my headache, so I stored it in my coat and left it inside.

If someone really needed me, I'd see them running.

"Well, the next time you decide to go remote, communicate that to your friend."

My friend?

"What are you—"

Graham. Of course.

"Sam went into to town, didn't she?" I ask.

Robins pulls one of the folded seats from the wall and props it up beside me. "Yes, and Graham apparently has the number of the general store. He's been calling the manager nonstop trying to get a hold of you."

If it were anyone else, I'd be worried. Since it's Graham, I don't even bother standing up to reach for the radio.

"Told Sam it's urgent and to get a hold of you as soon as possible."

"Did he use the whole 'worse than deforestation to an orangutan' bit?"

Dr. Robins laughs. "You know it."

That's one of the quirks about Graham. He binges animal documentaries and knows thousands of random facts to spew at the most unusual times.

Two words defined for Graham:

> **Dramatic**: intending or intended to create an effect; theatrical.
>
> **Exaggeration**: a statement that represents something as better or worse than it really is.

He's a dramatic exaggeration of a person.

I guarantee he's only calling because he's bored. Although, how he ever finds time to be bored between classes for his English education degree, shifts at Last Call, and spending time with Piper is beyond me.

He's dramatic, but he's also a workaholic. A dramatic workaholic.

I stand and head for the entrance of the building. "I'll ride into town later today. Is the car available?"

Robins starts to sort through the items on the table in front of her, finding a pair of gloves to slide on. "Paxton reserved the last one."

This makes me pause in the doorway. Something tells me it isn't Paxton who actually needs to go into town and the thought sends a weird shiver down my spine.

"I'm sure he wouldn't mind you tagging along. I think he's leaving in a few hours after Johnson comes back."

I don't nod or say anything in return. I'll stop him outside of the vehicle in a few hours and request a ride into town. Paxton isn't as overbearing as Graham can be, but he's certainly as generous. He'd give someone the shirt on his back if they needed it.

The polar opposite of his sister if the past few days are anything to go by. They couldn't be any more different from one another.

And yet, a part of me is suddenly looking forward to a ride into town. No better way to spend a forty-five-minute car ride than by getting under the skin of a woman who makes it so easy.

Normally, I'm not this much of a jerk. Jasmine tends to set me straight when my "mean side" as she calls it, comes out. But Jasmine is an ocean away and lighting a fire inside Camila is becoming my new favorite pastime.

Graham is the closest thing I have to a sibling. We went to the same school together and have been friends since the first grade.

I tended to keep to myself and avoid others, whereas Graham made it his personal mission to befriend every single person including me: the kid who wore dress clothes with a bow tie—not by choice—and had a seat reserved at the front of every class.

Mother made a call to the principal every school upgrade, ensuring I had the seat closest to the board and the teacher. I never raised my hand to answer questions, nor did I have trouble seeing with the glasses I'm prescribed. Mother wanted me to have every advantage available, despite that.

While other kids picked on me or hated me for the special attention I got, Graham always requested I sit next to him at lunch and tried to convince me to play tag with him at recess. When I ignored his recess requests and scurried off to the swings—an activity that is supposed to be solo—he trailed behind and sat on the swing next to me, talking my ear off.

This continued and we eventually became best friends.

He's the closest thing I've ever had to a brother. Maybe it's the fact that we aren't blood related, but the way Camila and Paxton behave with each other strikes my curiosity.

Along the entrance of the refuge outside the community building are the bickering siblings. Paxton is standing off to the edge of the only unreserved vehicle with his hands clasped in front of him like he's praying. Camila stands opposite him with her hands on her hips and her back to me.

From this distance, I can't make out what they're saying, but I imagine he screwed up again. Although, she doesn't seem like the easiest person to please to begin with.

As I stride closer, I catch the end of Paxton's plea. "…just this once."

"I can't believe you're ditching me again, Pax. Didn't I come here to spend time with you? You said I needed to get over it. Stop living in the past. You promised this would be some grand vacation but so far, it's been nothing but disaster in every corner."

My ears perk up at her words. What happened in the past that warranted this trip? Why is she so distraught over being here?

It can't possibly all be over one relationship.

The thought makes me cringe as I remember the exact reason I avoid going into town and picking up the phone as much as I possibly can.

It's my fault really, but this is all a means to an end.

"Look," Paxton steps closer to her, placing a hand on her shoulder. "I'm sorry, Camelot. I know I promised to spend time with you, and I will. It's just—"

"This is a once and a lifetime opportunity." The words are mimicked as she lets her hands fall to her sides and slowly turns away from him.

There's something lingering in her position as if there's so much more she wants to say but has no clue or enough time to lay it all out at his feet. It makes my chest ache.

It also allows me to realize I am still standing here, eavesdropping.

I clear my throat before either of them has the ability to dive into more personal information. Camila turns to face me, her already deflated expression turning into annoyance and irritation.

I consider lying that I didn't hear anything and pretend I just stumbled upon them. But she won't believe me even if I have the best poker face. So I shove my hands in the pocket of my jeans.

Paxton's gaze falls on me and his features turn hopeful. "Jay! Perfect timing. Any chance you're heading into town?"

Ignoring Camila staring daggers my way, I nod. "I was about to ask you the same thing."

"We were going to, but Liam is travelling a little North toward the village a few miles away and needs someone to tag along for photos."

And there it is. He needs to work, and she is too much of a spoiled brat to understand that. Even if he convinced her to travel here, did she really think he would drop everything and be at her beck and call?

Something I'm quickly learning about Camila: she's self-absorbed or...

<table><tr><td>Egotistical: excessively conceited or absorbed in oneself.</td></tr></table>

"Do you mind?" Paxton asks, bringing me back to the present.

I glance between the pair, Camila with her arms crossed over an ACDC t-shirt and Paxton with his camera already in hand, not having a clue what Paxton said.

Hesitantly, I nod.

He grabs my arm, ever the affectionate type, attempts to plant a sloppy kiss on my cheek, and continuously repeats "thank you" when I dodge his efforts.

A light chuckle echoes from the side of us, and I see Camila standing with an amused grin. Apparently, my discomfort is a form of quality entertainment.

He holds the key out to me, which I take without a second thought, and says, "I owe you big time."

Then, he turns back to his sister. He stands still for a few seconds as she stares at him. When she rolls her eyes and offers a small smile, he advances on her, wrapping her in the biggest hug. "You're the best. I promise I will make it up to you."

She fights in his hold, tapping his sides, but I can tell it's all pretend. She's holding back a laugh at his actions.

It makes me wonder which side of her is the front. The one full of curses and annoyed eyebrow raises, or the one she's wearing now. The one where she seems perfectly content despite the sweat at her hair line and the disappointment she keeps facing.

Paxton releases her, grabs a bag from the ground and rushes off in another direction. He walks backwards to yell at her, "Order more of those cookies. Use my card."

"I don't have your card, Pax," she calls back.

"It's the one in your Amazon account." He grins wickedly before running away.

Camila watches him saunter away, disbelief shining brightly on her face. She mumbles something under her breath, inaudible to me.

I'm an only child, but I can kind of relate to her frustrations because of Graham. He's like an annoying little brother who wants to be a part of everything.

He goes to the endless galas and parties Mother throws, taking over the socializing part and reintroducing me to the many guests I don't remember the name of. I help him afford medical bills and ensure he maintains regular checkups. I also provide the greatest and most constructive advice.

Despite how good of friends we are, he grates my nerves like a bee continuously buzzing at my ear that I can't swat away no matter how hard I try.

I head towards the vehicle and ask Camila, "You ready to go, Bell?"

It's the nickname I gave her last night. With how much she uses her expressions, words, and lack of intimate touch, as well as the way she always seems to start a fight—take now for example—there was only one name that filtered through my mind. That, and I had been skimming the 'B' section of the dictionary earlier that day. All of the rest I spurted just to mess with her.

"That's not my name." She opens the passenger door and climbs inside before slamming it shut.

I stare at her fuming through the window, shaking my head.

There is only a month left here, and this is how I'm going to spend it? Dealing with a woman who is constantly hot and cold?

The plan was for three months in Sub-Saharan Africa as a part of the volunteer medical team to learn and grow a name for myself outside of Mother. It's supposed to be a break from reality and my last independent experience before I go back to the city.

It's meant to be a time away and in nature, where it's quiet.

The last month here isn't supposed to consist of a woman who disrupts the peace.

Camila is stewing in her seat with her arms crossed over her chest and her jaw set.

This should be a fun ride.

CHAPTER EIGHT

CAMILA

"Would you say the air is more crisp or taught?" Lily asks through the landline perched against my ear.

Doc brought me to a general store in the town—apparently, the only place with a phone and cell service—after a very awkward and tense forty-five-minute car ride.

If he hadn't continued to call me by such a ridiculous name or eavesdrop on my personal conversation with Paxton, I might have been courteous enough to produce polite small talk. But he woke up and chose to be an ass today. Every day, actually, of the three days I've been here so far.

Three days in and twenty-seven more days to go.

Fucking perfect.

"Never mind," Lily continues before I have a chance to respond. "Hot air would be described differently."

I called to let her know I made it and am as safe as I possibly can be in this territory, which lasted a whole of twenty seconds before she started interrogating me.

She's been requesting as many descriptive details of the refuge as possible as inspiration for her book.

What is the scenery like?

Is there any wildlife?

Is the army there?

Or the military?

Maybe a mafia?

The questions just keep coming. Perks of being friends with a writer, I guess.

"Why not use 'humid' or 'sultry'?" I offer.

She makes an excited hum through the phone. "Humid is too generic, but I like sultry."

"What exactly are you writing about again?"

"A queen and her dragon romance. It will become a new classic. I guarantee it."

I read a few pages of Lily's stories before, but had to put it down the second certain phrases were used that left very little to the imagination and put images in my head I will never be able to erase.

Lily asked me to review one of her stories once in college. After reading the first chapter and mentioning the lack of action and abundance of dimples, smirks, and other confusing traits on a male, she never asked for me to read anymore of her works and I never offered.

Her genre of writing is not my cup of tea, but she has a wide fanbase. Or so she tells me.

"Weren't you just in the middle of a princess and a monster romance?" I loop my finger through the cord of the phone.

"Published it last week." By publish she means posting it to her blog. "Stay with me, Cam."

The door to the store opens back up, Doc stepping inside. When we arrived, I immediately went to the phone, thankful there's enough of a connection for me to at least find Lily's phone number in my phone to call and let her know I'm safe.

Doc, on the other hand, disappeared. I watched him grab a few things from the shelves, pay for them, and then slither back outside.

I'm not sure how much time passed, but enough for the snacks he grabbed to no longer be in his hands.

"So," Lily starts, "tell me about the rest of your trip. Did Paxton show you the surprise yet?"

This throws me. Not only do I know of no surprise, but Lily and Paxton despise each other. Paxton thinks she's a horrible friend and Lily hates him because…well, just because. She doesn't need a reason.

They have never actually met in person or talked on the phone and only know each other through me. I've combed my memory countless times to try and find what it is I described about each of them that made the other decide their intolerance but came up empty.

"What surprise?" I ask.

"Oh, you know, the one that involves the real reason you flew across the globe for an entire month."

I sigh, closing my eyes. Lily doesn't know what happened with Ben. She doesn't know I've been lying in bed anytime I don't have to be outside. She hasn't noticed how much I grow cold at someone else's touch.

If I didn't consider her a friend, I might even think she's been oblivious enough to not realize how much I've pulled away from *her* over the past year. But I know that's not the truth.

She still invites me out on the town when she's celebrating a breakthrough in one of her stories or needs new inspiration. There have been countless texts and calls from her on my phone daily: some funny videos online, some random thoughts or polite small talk, and demands for me to get up and go out.

I do. Sometimes. It's hard to say "no" to Lily, especially when she doesn't deserve to lose a friend who is also lying to her. But more times than not, I find any excuse I can to not accept her invitations.

A month away in some foreign place poses as the best excuse as of yet.

"I know you're in between jobs and stuff," Lily continues, "but you have to admit it's a little surprising you willingly got up and left for an entire month. I mean, you don't even like to go out to a sit-down restaurant because it requires more than thirty minutes of your time."

I don't, but for an entirely different reason. Restaurants are often filled with families and happy couples on a date. They showcase everything I ever wanted with Ben and everything I could never have. *Will* never have.

"I just wanted to spend some time with my brother, is all, Lil."

My attention snags on Doc, who's still standing by the doorway, leaning against the wall with his arms crossed. He's watching me with an expressionless face.

Does he do that often?

I wonder how many women have requested a restraining order against him for his blatant staring.

Something stirs inside me from his presence.

"I have to go," I whisper to Lily, cupping the bottom of the phone in the process.

"Call me at any time. You know where to find me."

I hang up the phone without so much as a goodbye from either of us. That's not something Lily and I do.

When the phone clicks back into its holder on the wall, I turn slowly to the man watching me by the door. I'm not sure how much of the conversation he heard between me and Paxton, but he got a glimpse into my life either way.

Paxton was supposed to bring me into town so I could contact Lily, and he could show me around. He has a job here, so I don't expect him to drop everything for me. If he has to do something, he has to do it, and that's the end of it.

But that doesn't mean I'm not going to give him crap for ditching me after his endless promises to hang out. It also doesn't mean that Doc has the right to give me those judgmental looks he's been sending my way ever since.

Running on pure irritation, I stride towards him. He doesn't even flinch as I approach. "I'm ready to go whenever you're done staring, Doc."

He pushes off the wall, staring down to meet my gaze as he reaches his full height. "It's Jason. How else was I supposed to know when you're done with the phone?"

Then, he saunters away to the landline. I stand mute for a moment, watching him dial a number and place the device close to his ear.

From this distance, I can't hear a word he utters, and his back is turned to me so reading his expression is off the table too.

Releasing a long exhale, I decide to scavenge through the short aisles and see what there is. It's not a store you'd find in New York City. Where we have loads of snacks and junk food, this store has an abundance of canned food and cheap medical supplies.

It's one of few buildings in the town and each is spaced relatively apart. They are the size of a convenience store too, rather than the larger buildings on the refuge. There are no signs hanging on any verandas—partially because there are no verandas—and the places aren't close enough for a sidewalk to be leading from one to the next.

I pick up a pair of socks. Then set it down. Pick up a can of chicken noodle soup with no brand name. Then set it down. This process continues as I move through the aisles, slowly getting closer and closer to Doc.

He hung up a moment ago only to redial the phone and whisper in it. I know he's whispering because I'm within six feet of him now and his words are indistinguishable.

I'm not eavesdropping. This is a small space and if I happen to be within hearing distance, it's not my fault.

But when I brush past him to leave and wait outside, I catch wind of the end of his sentence.

"...three weeks."

I slow my pace without thinking.

"Use the card I gave you to withdraw money for the deposit."

Deposit? What is he paying for?

Is he buying a house in the middle of nowhere? No, there's no house within a fifty-mile radius.

A car maybe?

He must be doing business for some other location.

I'm almost at the door when the phone clicks against its frame. I turn to find Doc with his jaw set and a frown on his lips.

Maybe he's not buying anything. Isn't someone supposed to be ecstatic when they purchase something? Then again, I despise watching money drain from my account as if it physically hurts me.

Doc comes towards me. Without making eye contact, he opens the door to the store, and asks, "You ready?"

He doesn't seem like the type to be all sunshine and rainbows, but even I can tell something isn't right.

I want to open my mouth and ask. Bottling things up or not having someone to lay everything on is one of the toughest things we do as humans. When everything happened with Ben, I had Paxton, but even that was short lived. My brother, as wonderful as he is, can only do so much.

He can't hold me at night when all of the insecurities and doubts come flooding in to keep me awake. He doesn't know when my smile doesn't reach my eyes or when I'm faking a laugh.

I can tell him anything I want, show him how my arms shake from the load they're holding, but he can't carry it for me.

Paxton doesn't understand why I was even in a relationship with Ben to begin with, let alone why a part of me almost wishes I never caught him cheating.

If I hadn't walked in on him and Elizabeth, we might still be together. Yeah, I might still be tucked in the shadows with him, but we'd still be dating.

Touching.

Even if he's a liar and a cheat and I'm supposedly better off without him, he still knew how I liked to be held when the rest of the world seemed to cave in.

"Yeah," I answer Doc, "Let's go.

CHAPTER NINE

JASON

"Who's hungry?" Johnson yells at the small group of us as he opens the door to the dining hall.

We can come in here to eat at any time, but we all generally end up eating together because of the schedules.

A few of the nurses push past his excited stance and into the dining hall for food. Spending a day in the sun treating a large group of people can make you starve.

So much so that you don't become your best self. Sam and a few others start filling in at the tables and diving into the food without so much as a "please" or pause.

I can't say I blame them since my stomach has been growling for the past hour, but I try to go in with a little more restraint.

The second I step inside, the air is charged with some type of electricity. Something pulls me towards the left where none other than the woman with a short bob of black hair and tan skin sits at the table beside her brother.

We haven't seen each other for a few days, both deciding to keep our distance from each other after going to town. She finds me annoying, and I find her insufferable.

It'd be a lie to say I haven't noticed her around the refuge, though. True to his word, Paxton has been showing her around and introducing her to some of the residents. He picked up on the native language a lot quicker than I did.

If I remember correctly, he once said he knows five languages. When Paxton is passionate about something, he doesn't let anything get in his way. Even if that means entertaining his sister, apparently.

She's smiling at something he and his boss, Liam, are chatting about. When either of them looks at her, she grins wider and laughs a soundless laugh, but the second they turn away her joy drops.

It even to someone who doesn't know her, her expressions are so obviously:

> **Fake**: forge or counterfeit.
> **Feign**: pretend to be affected by a feeling, state, or injury.
> **Pretend**: speak or act so as to make it appear that something is the case when in fact it is not.

These words cycle in my mind as I observe the trio, my eyes mostly staying locked on Camila. She must sense me staring because she turns her head towards me and offers me the same forced smile she gave them.

I hate it.

Worse: I hate that I hate it.

These types of things aren't usually noticeable to me and after the way I left things in the city, the last thing I should be doing is noticing the tells of a beau—

My teeth clench together as I open and close my fists to counteract the odd pinch in my chest.

"Would you like to join, Doc?" Camila asks me with her fork dangling from between her fingers.

There's no doubt in my mind it's sarcasm, but it only spurs me on more.

"Oh," Paxton starts to answer for me, but I sit down in the only empty spot—directly beside Camila-before he can finish. "Jay is sitting with us, I guess."

Paxton and many of the others have invited me to eat with them multiple times. I said no to each one.

Socializing isn't my thing. I much prefer the corner of the room where I can avoid all of the usual pleasantries and having to apologize for forgetting someone's name.

At Mother's galas, I tend to stride towards the furthest table and set up shop. Since it'd be rude to write a dissertation or do research in the middle of an event, I pull up the dictionary on my phone and just scroll through.

There's a dictionary I keep in my room to highlight any words that stick out to me. It's an anxiety relieving trick I've done for as long as I can remember.

I used to fiddle with stress balls or other things to keep my mind busy like trying out for the baseball team. Neither pleased Mother, though. Reading a dictionary, on the other hand, would put me above my peers.

"My name is Jason," I remind Camila. I don't know why she keeps forgetting that.

"Why is my brother so surprised you sat down?" Camila whispers to me.

I look over her head at her brother. He, along with the few other people around, has their eyes trained on me.

I lean back and sigh.

You accept one invitation to sit and suddenly the whole world has flipped upside down.

"Juvenile," I mumble under my breath.

Camila releases a small laugh, and it warms my insides. One small sound and my ears have perked up waiting for the next one.

How do I get another one?

"Are you going to eat?" Paxton asks me. "Or continue staring at my little sister?"

I don't miss the warning he puts into the words, nor do I miss the purposeful use of "little".

There is nothing little about Camila. If she were the weather, she'd be a tornado sweeping up and blowing all rational thought away.

"Here," a familiar female voice comes from the right of me as a plate filled with potatoes, roast, and cooked carrots appears in front of me. "I made you a plate."

"Thanks, Sam," I nod to her as I slowly take it from her hands.

"Of course. We all know how hangry you can get."

A snort comes from my left. I'm in between two completely different women and the one who has my full attention is the one who doesn't want it.

"There's an extra seat by me…" Sam points a thumb to a table on the other end of the room where the rest of the nurses are sitting. "If you want to join, that is."

I've turned her down before. Too many times to count. And yet, she doesn't seem to get the hint. "I'm alright here," is all I offer before digging into the food and removing my attention from her.

A hard stare burns into me from the left as Sam stutters out, "Oh, okay. Of course. Enjoy your meal."

When she disappears and the heat of Camila's stare becomes too much for me to endure, I say, "What?" It's more of a statement than it is a genuine question.

If she thinks she's going to start lecturing about my manners, she has another thing coming.

"You shouldn't lead her on, you know," Camila snarkily adds as she shuffles her own food around her plate.

"All I said was 'thank you'."

"You should have said 'no thanks'. You give women the wrong idea when you blindly accept our kindness."

I set my fork down. "Women or you, Camila?"

There's no memory of the kindness she's shown me in the past week, but something tells me her annoyance has little to actually do with Sam. Especially since she *doesn't know us.*

"Please, don't go getting a big head."

"I don't think I am. I think you're upset I didn't blatantly turn Sam down and I want to know why."

She crosses her arms, huffing out a breath.

Of all the childish and bratty ways to be, she sure wears them all like they are the finest clothing. My blood boils with irritation as she doesn't bother answering me.

"Why did you even ask me to sit down in the first place if you were going to be like this?"

It hasn't gone out of my notice that the other people at the table are watching us and waiting to see what happens next. I could care less about what they all think, though.

Hell, I should care less about what this insufferable woman thinks.

One moment you think she's nice and the next—

"I didn't realize how much of a douche you were when I offered."

A douche?

I'm about to stand and forget dinner altogether, maybe throw a few curses in her direction in the process, when another voice breaks into our disagreement.

"Camelot," Paxton says softly, "that was a bit harsh, don't you think?"

"You mean it's okay for a man to lead someone on?"

"That's not what I'm saying, and you know it. Jay can't help if someone likes him."

She takes this information in, her arms loosening around her chest before falling to pick her fork back up again.

"Maybe you should apologize," Paxton whispers to her, but it's audible to everyone at the table. I also watch him raise his sheepish, apologetic eyes to me after giving Camila a stern glare.

This should be fun.

Camila twists in her seat to face me. "I'm not sorry about what I said. You should make your feelings clear no matter what the circumstances are."

I completely agree with her, but I'm not going to tell her that. I'm also not going to mention that I've rejected Sam multiple times before. She knows very clearly where I stand.

Does that stop her advancements? Apparently not.

Paxton must poke her back because she leans forward a little before sending a glare over her shoulder at him.

I bite back the laughter stewing inside me.

"But I shouldn't have called you a douche." She mumbles something else under her breath, probably taking it all back, but I don't catch it.

"Is that sarcasm?" I never know how to tell these things. Usually, Graham has to signal to me with a shake of his head when I take someone too seriously.

She lifts her gaze to meet mine and I see the first genuine emotion on her face. It's a scowl, probably not the most enticing to receive, but I find the irritation bubbling inside me start to simmer.

"No, Doc. It's not sarcasm."

She turns back to her food, and so does everyone else, forgetting about the display she just created.

It is only going to prove her theory about me being a douche even more, but I find myself inching a hair closer to her. It's as if now that my body has discovered her, it can't go with being further than a foot from her.

If she notices my movements, she doesn't say anything.

We all continue to eat, Paxton and Liam discussing their photos while Camila occasionally adds in a word or two. Sometimes, the siblings mention a moment from their past.

Camila brings up a time when Paxton didn't believe ducks were real because his collection of rubber ducks looked different.

Paxton counters her memory with one of when Camila stacked books and boxes on top of a chair to try and reach a container of cookies their mom hid only for the pile to topple underneath her and her to scrape her arm off the counter.

I find myself wanting to see the scar, the evidence of her past.

Those are the stories I tune into. The rest of the time, I observe the woman beside me, learning her tells and scouring my brain for ways to earn another one of those laughs.

And only once, when my knee accidentally brushes against hers and an electric shock jolts through me, am I reminded of Jasmine and the promise I made.

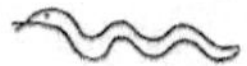

It'd be nice to say sleep has trouble finding me even when I'm home and in my own bed, but that'd be a lie. I haven't been able to shut my body off for longer than a few hours before I'm up and thinking.

Thinking about the promises I made and the future I will have to uphold when I get back home.

My legs start to stiffen beneath me as the wooden bench numbs my senses. The discomfort is minor to the raging thoughts my mind sifts through.

Jasmine's professional, but friendly demeanor as she scribbled in her notebook at Graham and I's kitchen table. Mother's excited shriek and tight hug when I told her the news. Father's pat on the back.

It all focuses in and out in front of me like the worst montage.

"Please tell me you're not married."

The request nearly makes me jump from my spot on one of the benches outside the camp as Camila plops down beside me.

It's dark with the night cloaking us, but the large hoodie around her body is visible enough to send a weird image in my mind of her in one of my hoodies.

I shake the thoughts away and raise a brow at her.

She gestures to my hands. I've been fiddling with my left ring finger, too lost in thought to even notice until she mentioned it.

Shaking my head, "No." But I imagine it's not too far in the future.

"Were you?" she tries instead.

"Unless you count my mother's fantasies, no."

"Mom set you up on blind dates?"

"More like has pushed me towards the daughter of one of her friends since the day I was born."

I don't know what makes me open up, and to the same woman who gave me the stink eye while I saved her life no more than a week ago, but the truths continue to fall from me.

"If she could have forged a marriage contract, I'm sure she would have."

Camila tilts her head at me. "I'm assuming you aren't interested in her?"

No. I'm not.

If I'm being honest, Jasmine and I shared a moment once. It was our junior year in high school and our parents didn't give us an option in taking anyone else to the prom.

We were to be each other's date in all events. Jasmine and I, fed up with everything, decided to just roll with it.

"I know we have no romantic interest in each other, but I would love to have at least one romantic night of my teen life," she pleaded as we entered the school gymnasium.

I don't remember the color dress she wore that night, but I'm sure it was something elegant and modest. I'm sure it also matched the tie to my suit.

"Are you asking me to act like this is a real date?" I studied the black and red decorations lining the walls.

"Of course not. That would be ridiculous. But could you, out of the kindness of your black heart—" I narrowed my eyes at her when she said this— "pretend you don't hate me?"

"I don't hate you."

"Jason, you haven't even looked at me since the moment you picked me up tonight. Do you even know what color my dress is?"

When I turned to look at her, she covered my eyes with her manicured hands.

"Without looking."

"Blue?" I guessed.

She sighed and let her hand fall from my face.

I was wrong. "Look, I may not *stare*—"

"I didn't ask you to stare."

"—at you, but that doesn't mean I hate you. I simply hate the fact that our parents pin us with each other."

"Maybe there's a reason."

I laughed. Loud enough to gain the attention of some of our peers.

"See why I assume you hate me?" She crossed her arms.

"I'm sorry," I said, but the laughter still found a way to come through. "I'm not laughing at you, it's just—you can't be serious."

"We never actually tried to like each other before. We just refused to even acknowledge one another from the moment we were smart enough to know what they were doing."

I sobered at this. "What are you saying Jaz?"

"Let's try. Just for tonight. Let's put the whole marriage thing behind and just pretend for one second that we are normal teenagers."

The idea was foreign to me in all aspects. We were the top of our class and participated in every club, including student government. We didn't have hobbies because we didn't have the free time to invent one.

Normal teenagers are something we have never been. Normal is a word I'm not sure even exists in my vocabulary. And I had the word underlined and annotated in the dictionary the school provided.

I ran a hand through my hair as I considered. Jasmine was beautiful and the center of every guy's fantasy. You could hear as much just from passing the locker room.

And she was supposed to be my future wife.

If everyone else, including our parents, saw a future for us, why couldn't I?

"Just for tonight?" I asked.

"Yes. Then you can get back to hating me like you do."

"I don't hate you."

"Fine, strongly dislike."

I shoved my hands in my pocket and stared at the crowd around us. Students were shouting, singing, grinding against one another, slipping a few drinks in in the process, while we stood at the entrance.

"What do normal teenagers do?" I turned back to her, hoping she didn't suggest any of that.

She looked disgusted, but she swallowed it. "Dance."

"I'm not dancing like *that.*"

"One night, Jason." She grabbed my hand and dragged me to the dance floor.

Luckily, it transitioned to a slow song the second we stopped. She positioned our hands so mine were on her hips and hers were wrapped around my neck.

"This isn't how you waltz," I reminded her.

"*Normal* teens," *she* reminded *me*. "Just loosen up."

I tried, shrugging the tension out of my shoulders. I let my hands trace her thin fame and the smooth dress flowing from her skin. I tried to find a feeling emerging in my chest or even an animalistic one, but nothing surfaced.

My hands were too big for her frame, and she was nearly eye level with me. It didn't fit. *We* didn't fit.

"Jaz," I started to mumble. "I know you want me to pretend, but…"

She laid her head on my chest as the scent of her orange blossom shampoo floated to my nose. "You don't feel anything do you?"

I relaxed, wrapping my arms tighter around her to comfort her. It didn't escape my notice that nothing stirred to life inside me no matter how close we got to each other. "No. I'm sorry."

In a huff of breath, she released her arms from around my neck and took a step away from me. "I don't either."

"I'm sorry. I know you wanted tonight to just be a night of romance and I—"

She shook her head. "You can't force feelings. And all I could think the whole time was 'Jason Young is dancing with me, and I feel absolutely nothing'. If anything, I despise you for touching me."

It's a joke so I force a smile on my lips. "So, *you* hate *me*?"

"Wasn't that clear?" She asks it with the most innocent smile on her lips, but the cracks in the facade are visible. "I'm going to go find the spiked punch. And Graham."

"Why Graham?"

"Because, as insufferable as he is, he knows how to flirt."

"You like Graham?"

"God no, but he can at least make me feel *something*."

From anyone else, it may have felt like an insult. From Jasmine, it only felt like an inside joke.

No matter how hard we tried, we just couldn't force ourselves to like each other. We are two puzzle pieces meant for different puzzles. At least, until someone cuts the pieces to fit the puzzle a little bit better.

"No," I answer Camila's question in the present. "I'm not."

Time changes things, though, I guess.

CHAPTER TEN

CAMILA

I tilt my head at the man beside me and ask, "I'm assuming you aren't interested in her?"

Doc is silent for a moment as he continues to circle his ring finger with the fingers of his other hand. It's a nervous tick I've seen him do randomly. In the dining hall, outside the medical building, just sitting on one of the benches.

It wasn't my intention to find him and start up a conversation, but it's already one in the morning and I can't fall asleep for the life of me. I decided to take a walk and found him sitting on the bench outside of the medical building.

I figured he could either bore me enough to fall asleep or irritate me enough for me to occupy my mind instead of the other man filling the spaces in my brain.

What I didn't expect was to find him depressed and thinking of marriage. Or a possible marriage, I guess.

Mom never pushed me to date so I have no idea what this feeling must be like for him. I imagine it's not something to be ecstatic about. Although maybe if our parents were in charge of our love lives, we wouldn't be prone to falling for the wrong guy.

"No," Doc finally responds to my question, filling the empty night with his gravelly voice. "I'm not."

"Have you told her that?"

He turns to look at me and scoffs. "Which one?"

I roll my eyes. "Either. Both."

"Yeah. They both are well aware how I feel about the situation."

"That's good, right? Gets them off your back." Surely his mother can't force him down the aisle.

He doesn't respond, just stares out into the darkness ahead of us. There are very few stars in the sky tonight. Only enough to create a small, jagged line.

Doc, however, seems to be counting hundreds of them with how focused he is on the endless sky.

I shift, deciding to stand and leave him alone with his thoughts, when he asks, "What about you?"

"What about me?"

"You married?"

The question sends my heart skydiving into my stomach. I was never one of the girls who dreamed of their wedding day. No boy ever made marriage seem like a big thing I just *had* to do.

Then I met Ben, and the wedding bells seemed to follow me everywhere. My Pinterest account is filled with boards of gowns, hairstyles, decorations, locations, first dance songs, and hundreds of other ideas.

I thought he might even pop the question after the publicity stunt with Elizabeth ended when he showed me a part of his past.

He didn't open up about himself much, but three months before everything happened, he exposed me to a side of him the rest of the world never got to see.

"Ben," I whisper-yelled as we cut across the parking lot with the dark night shadowing us from any witnesses. "Where are we going?"

He held my hand tighter as he guided us toward a building. "I want to show you something."

The building said "Sunny Orphanage" on the front and loomed over us like a curse.

"Are we breaking and entering?"

He looked back at me with a smirk on his lips. "Where's the fun in me telling you that?"

If I didn't know him and his usual playful personality, I would be worried. Instead, I shook my head as my long hair hid the blush on my cheeks.

He took us to the playground on the side and motioned for me to sit on one of the swings. My skin stuck to the plastic as soon as I did.

"Why are we here, Ben?" I asked when he didn't say a word, but he just sat motionless on the swing beside me.

"I grew up here." His voice was rough as if he were speaking the memories into existence. "My parents gave me up when they had me and this is where I came."

I looked over the place again as I envisioned a smaller Ben, one with the curly hair I suspect he had, running around the grass and playing like a normal kid. Not hiding in the shadows like the man he is now.

"This place," he grabbed my hands in his, pulling my swing closer to his. "It's special to me. I've never brought or told anyone else about it before."

The idea of finally being the first witness to something in his life made me melt before him. I would have given him everything at that moment because of him sharing something so precious to me.

"I know keeping us a secret can be hard, but here, we don't have to worry about the paparazzi or anyone recognizing us. Here," one of his hands found the side of my face. I leaned into his touch. "We can just be us."

It sounded so lovely. A place where we didn't have to hide in the shadows was something I craved for so long I forgot what the sun felt like against my skin.

He leaned in, his mouth a hair away from mine. I placed a hand on his chest before he could get any closer, "What if someone sees?"

Even in the dark I could see the smile on his lips. "No one can see us, Camila." Then, his lips found mine and I let every other worry fade away.

Now, I sit in the dark with a different man. One who for some reason doesn't make me feel like I'm hiding, but like I'm resting before the sun rises.

"No," I answer Doc about whether or not I'm married. "Not the marrying type."

"Does it have anything to do with the recent breakup?"

My blood turns cold. How in the hell does he...?

"It's not difficult to put two and two together. Especially after that incident at dinner." He stretches his legs out in front of him. "It's either that or something worse."

I squint my eyes at him. Never has he met me or heard about me before I landed here a little over a week ago, and yet he has figured out the one thing I have kept hidden from everyone.

"You don't have to tell me," he adds after a moment as he rubs at the back of his neck. "I understand wanting to keep your privacy."

He's giving me an out. An opportunity to call it a night and head back to Paxton's tent to forget our talk and sleep the rest of the night away.

It's what I should do. Especially since he's the same man who irritates me almost as much as Paxton.

But something keeps me glued to the bench as I lean back and settle in. Maybe it's because he opened up to me earlier or maybe I'm out of it from a lack of sleep, but I tell him the one thing I can't bring myself to tell even Lily. It's not like I'll ever see him again after I leave here anyway and telling someone the one thing I've had locked in a box for years is too appealing to keep my mouth shut.

"I'm a stunt double."

His brows pinch together in confusion, but he doesn't say a word.

"He...he's an actor. We worked on the same set about two or three years ago and—well, we became a bit of a thing. There was no rule against us dating, but he and the lead actress had a publicity deal to pretend to be a couple in public."

I keep my attention on the slippers on my feet as I toe the ground beneath me. Doc is still studying me, but his gaze isn't burning me. It's...encouraging me. Like he genuinely wants to hear everything I have to say.

"So we hid our relationship. From everyone. Two years went by, and the contract ended. I bought tickets for a vacation to surprise him since we could finally be a couple in public."

I almost laugh at the memory. I set a reminder and five alarms on my phone to make sure I booked the trip at just the right time to get the perfect discount.

"When I went to his apartment to surprise him..." I release a long exhale. "Let's just say he was occupied."

"It wasn't..."

"The lead actress?" I fill in for him. "Would it make it any better if it wasn't?"

It's one of many questions I have been asking myself nonstop. If it weren't Elizabeth underneath him, but some other woman, would I have forgiven him?

Would I be on a trip with him instead of at this refuge?

It's a question I will never have the answer to.

"Actors are assholes," Doc mutters. He doesn't say sorry or give me a pitiful look. Instead, he makes me smile and I couldn't be more grateful.

"Not all of them. Just Ben."

"God, his name is Ben?"

I nod.

"You should've known from that alone how much of a douche he is."

"What do you have against Bens'?"

"You mean, besides the fact that their named after a big clock tower? Well, every Ben I know has cheated."

Curious, I sit up straighter. "How many Bens do you know?"

"Two. One from middle school who constantly peeked at my tests when he thought I wasn't looking. I purposely wrote the wrong answer on a few for him to copy, then corrected them in the last minute of the exam."

I laugh. "And the second? What did he do?"

I'm still grinning when he turns his full attention to me. His gaze is locked with mine and his hands are on his lap, but I feel like he's caressing every part of me. "He was dumb enough to cheat on a woman any man would love to just hold the hand of."

Something flutters in my chest as the chill dissipates from my body. I duck my head; thankful he can't see the blush on my cheeks.

He was talking about me, right? Or does he know of another Ben who cheated?

"We should get to bed," he says, but doesn't make a move to stand.

"Thank you."

"For what?"

"Letting me dive into my whole pitiful life story to you."

He shifts to face me completely, his knee brushing mine and sending an electric bolt through me. "Your life isn't pitiful, Bell."

His sincerity makes me melt so I latch onto something else instead. "That's not my name."

"It's your nickname."

"Fine. But why Bell?"

He shakes his head, standing and stretching his arms above his head. "I believe I'm the only one who needs to know that."

It's just a nickname so I shouldn't care this much, but I do. Or maybe it's the sudden burst of energy this conversation has given me.

I stand, shoving my hands in the pocket of Paxton's hoodie. "How about we call a truce?"

"A truce?"

"Yeah. We'll put the past in the past."

He crosses his arms. "Does that mean you won't give me anymore of those looks?"

I narrow my eyes at him with a frown. "What look?"

"That one. The one that makes me feel guilty."

I hold my hand out to him in an offer of a handshake. "Fine. I won't give you that look, so long as you don't deserve it."

"Deal." He places his palm in mine. It sends warmth through my fingers and up my arm.

Quickly, I pull from his touch and deposit my burning hand back into my pocket. "Now tell me about the nickname."

He starts to back away. "No can do."

"We shook on it."

"No, we shook on a truce in which I won't receive any of those annoyed looks from you."

"Doc—"

"Jason."

"I'm not going to call you that unless you tell me what the hell it means."

He laughs. It's soft and beautiful enough to make me consider telling him never mind.

"Good night, Bell," is the last thing he says before heading back to his own bed.

Chapter Eleven

CAMILA

It has been nine days since I first arrived here, meaning there are twenty-one days left. As much as this place seems to taunt me, I find myself wanting it to last longer if only to stave off the time of my return.

When I get home, I will have no job to busy myself with. Instead, I will be transported right back to where I started by having an empty studio apartment to barricade myself in for the foreseeable future.

Maybe I can convince Lily I'm staying here longer so she won't come knocking on the door and demanding to see me. She means well, but sometimes having to be around people is too much. Usually, it's simpler with Lily than others because she distracts and takes the heat off of heavy topics.

We don't talk about my things, nor do we talk about hers. It's one of the things I admire most about our friendship.

There was a time in college when my scholarships fell through, and I had to start using student loans. Lily found me wallowing in our dorm room with a blanket over my head and the curtains shut.

She didn't berate me for answers or demand I get some vitamin D. Instead, she told me she was having writers block, and we needed to go out for her to gain some inspiration.

So I forced myself out of bed and she dressed me up in one of her tight dresses.

We didn't talk about my problems once that night. Back then, I thought it might have been because she didn't care enough to tell I wasn't okay. But as our friendship grew and those occurrences happened more and more often—she would suddenly hit a snag during an intense writing session or suddenly hit a major breakthrough in the middle of tearing a work apart—I knew it was for me.

She let me use her problems to escape mine and it's one of the things I admire most about Lily.

Paxton, on the other hand, finds it selfish and believes I'm thinking too much into her self-absorbed ways.

Right now, for example, he's reminding me of a time Lily brought me to see one of Ben's movies when I was wallowing in bed about him.

"She doesn't know about him, Pax," I call to him.

We're outside near one of the resident's homes for him to take a few pictures of the lack of vegetation. I've gone with him a few times on his previous adventures, but this is the first one we've started to talk during it.

Usually, he focuses on his task while speaking to the residents to make sure he does the issue justice. Today, though, there aren't as many people around and he seems particularly chatty.

So, I parked myself on a spot on the dirt, leaning back on my hands with my legs crossed, as Paxton moves around in front of me to capture the best photographs he can.

"How do you know?" he asks me. "She could secretly know about the two of you and was jealous you were dating a movie star, so she rubbed it in your face."

"First off, we aren't in middle school. And secondly, Lily isn't like that. What do you have against her anyway? You've never met her before."

He shrugs. "Don't need to. From your stories I can tell the two of us wouldn't get along."

The only reason they wouldn't get along is because of their undying, but misplaced, hate for one another.

"Tell me about Maya," I request of him in hopes of steering the conversation somewhere not on me.

Maya is one of the residents here. Paxton talks to her the most and turns a deep shade of pink when she looks in his direction.

"What about her?" He visibly stiffens at my question.

I grin. "You like her."

"Do not."

"Oh, so your camera roll isn't mostly comprised of her?"

He adjusts the camera lens, turning his back to me. "She's a good model."

I chuckle a little. Paxton has never been good at flirting games. It takes a special kind of woman to fall for his nerdy personality.

There was this girl he went to high school with— Piper, I think her name is—and they were the best of friends. He used to skip his math class just to have the same study period as her. They would sit in the school library together and talk about the most random and unknown things.

He asked her out once, she said no, and he continued to stay her friend in hopes he could change her mind. When graduation rolled around, he scooped her up in his arms and asked her again.

She rejected him. I still cringe at the memory of watching it all happen as I stood with our parents a few feet away from it.

"Camila, remind me to make some leche fritas when we get home," Mother told me as we watch Paxton slowly set Piper back on the ground.

"He's going to need more than dessert to get over that girl," my father sighed.

He did. Mom went through countless baking frenzies trying to keep up with the increase in his sweet tooth. He gained at least twenty pounds in his freshman year of college.

Joining the school track team, though, when he had a crush on some girl named Haylee, helped him lose it all. He never worked up the courage to ask her out so there haven't been any more sugar binges since Piper. None that I've been aware of at least, but I also haven't been around him as often as I used to.

"You have no right to grill me," Paxton from the present warns, "when you've been flirting with a certain doctor."

I scoff. "Flirting? Please. We've merely called a truce."

"Looks like an awfully cozy truce to me."

Since our chat the other night, Doc has taken our truce to heart. We nod and smile at one another in passing.

I no longer run the other way when I see him approaching. He doesn't groan and roll his eyes when he notices me.

We aren't best friends, but we aren't enemies either. We are at a weird in between.

Paxton happened to notice me wave to Doc on our way out of the refuge this morning and hasn't shut up about it since. My kindness towards Doc is nothing more than being polite.

"I'm here to start fresh, Pax. Not jump into another relationship."

No matter how attractive the guy may be or how surprisingly easy it is to talk to him, I'm not going down that rabbit hole again. Not this soon.

I need to figure myself out first before I go on another date. When I am ready to date, it's certainly not going to be with Doc.

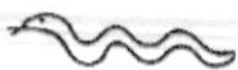

We come back to the camp a few hours before dusk, right around the time the last few stragglers enter the dining hall. Perfect timing for my growling stomach.

My only hope is there's enough left of the main dish for me to chow on, so I don't have to open one of those cans of soup.

The main meals aren't five stars or even two stars, but they are a heck of a lot better than processed soups.

"I'm going to go set my camera down and then I'll be there," Pax tells me before heading off to his tent.

When I step inside, I'm surprised to find a certain lone figure sitting at a table in the corner with a large book propped open in front of him.

Carefully, I sneak up to him as he drags a pencil across the page to underline something.

"Reading something interesting?" I whisper to him as I plop down in the seat beside him.

"Faffy," he says without turning to me.

I arch a brow. "Is that some fantasy term or something?"

"It's an adjective for something awkward or time consuming."

"You lost me."

He pushes the book towards me and that's when I see what he's reading. A dictionary. He's hunched over in the dining hall of a camp, annotating a dictionary.

And by the many scribbles on the page, this isn't his first read.

"Of all the things I expected you to be interested in, this was not top on the list."

He takes the book back, closing it, and meets my gaze. "Yeah? What were you expecting?"

"I don't know. Maybe history books. Superhero comics. Something rugged and masculine."

"The dictionary isn't masculine?" he teases.

"Oh no, it is. Don't worry, your masculinity is still in check."

He cracks a smile, and it sends a surge of warmth through me. I did that. I made his lips twist up.

Suddenly, I'm too aware of our proximity and the fact that my hand somehow found its way onto his shoulder. I pull away as if burned by his touch.

God, what is wrong with me?

He stands up and starts to leave, without picking up the full plate of food on the table.

"Hey," I stop him. "Aren't you going to eat."

He tucks the dictionary under his arm. "Truce, remember?"

Then, he saunters away.

I stare down at the plate, full of every item from the main meal, my mouth already salivating at the smell.

"They're all out," Paxton complains as he takes the spot Doc just vacated.

Digging into the food in front of me as I fight the grin on my lips, I say, "You snooze, you lose."

CHAPTER TWELVE

JASON

The ER is the place I always felt most at home and myself. The rush of bouncing from patient to patient, being the person someone relied on, meeting a variety of people; it's a feeling I crave.

Missing it and feeling lackluster is one of the things I worried about when I saw my name on the list to come here.

To prove my skills and abilities and not have my name tie to Mother, is the reason I requested to be on the list to begin with. It's my goal to open my own practice and find a way to offer healthcare to families with lesser income than the majority.

But that doesn't mean I haven't had my doubts. Mother is the reason I was accepted at the hospital. Hell, she's the reason I started thinking about being a doctor to begin with because of the medical toys she would buy me when I was a child.

She used to point a stern finger at me when I played action figures with Graham and Jasmine but placed her hands over her heart when I played doctor.

It's not just my dream, but hers. But what if the only reason I'm good at what I do or even get a foot in the door isn't because of my skills and passion, but because of Mother?

Father always made sure I knew of other careers. He would take me on trips to the museum to show me some of the lesser-known professions on display or would put on that *Dirty Jobs* show in the living room to expose me to things outside of Mother's hospital, and his bank, despite Mother's protests at watching such a thing.

"If you want to be a doctor, that's amazing," he told me. "But if you decide to go down a different path, like making jellybeans or working as a waiter, we'd still be proud of you and will support you the whole time."

My father's encouragement and blind faith in my abilities are some of the things that has solidified my passion in medicine. Even if Mother disapproved of me choosing a different path, Father would always have my back.

It was enough for me to know I chose this for myself. But now, at a hospital where everyone knows the director is my mother, it makes doubt nibble at the back of my mind.

Even at this camp, I'm working with a team who know my connections. This much is evident when Johnson mentions taking a break for the day to join one of the festivities in a nearby village. Everyone in the room turns to look at me, including Robins.

Feigning nonchalance and pretending like the entire world isn't on my back, I shrug. "As long as every patient has been seen today, I don't see why not."

A few fists pump the air, while others start to chat about who's riding with who since there's only four vehicles available.

I reach for the clipboard hanging on the wall, deciding to do rounds for the few patients who have to stay in the medical building due to injuries or illness, when Robins grabs it first.

"I will do rounds," she says with a stern look.

"I don't mind. You go with everyone else."

"Why? So you can be here alone to pout?"

I cross my arms over my chest. "I don't pout. And you and I both know you are the more sociable one between us."

"True but working all the time isn't healthy. And part of volunteering is being able to see other parts of the world. You, Young, have yet to so much as glimpse at the sun here."

That's an exaggeration if I've heard one.

She shoves at my chest. "Now go before I have Sam and Johnson tie you to a stretcher and roll you out."

The sound of drums fills the air as our group travels through the streets of the village and closer to a spot of a few people beating drums.

In front of them are women and men dressed in the brightest reds, yellows, and greens as they dance and sing to the music. A few onlookers and others dance off to the side or jump in to join the women.

It's an event full of life and laughter and everyone moves together.

Our group divides itself up between a few local food vendors lined up along the path and standing to watch the music.

I consider tucking myself in a corner to wait out the festival until everyone decides to drive back when my attention snags on Paxton snapping a few pictures with none other than a certain woman standing beside him.

She's watching the dance and smiling. A genuine smile. My heart leaps in my chest at the sight and I'm not sure why.

I'm not supposed to be drawn to her or any other woman for that matter. Especially since I will be on a flight to return home in less than three weeks.

Yet, I can't seem to stop myself from walking in that direction to come and stand beside her. "Do you like music?"

Do you like music? Seriously, that's what I come up with.

She peers up at me, the smile still bright on her face. It's like the sun has been hiding behind clouds all day and is finally peeking through, warming my skin at its touch.

Stop it, Jason.

"What are you doing here?" she asks.

I shove my hands into the pockets of my shorts. Changing out of my scrubs because of this heat is one of the best decisions I've made. "Group outing."

"I would have thought you would hideout in the medical building. Find some excuse to not socialize."

How is it she's only known me for less than two weeks and she can read me like a book?

All of the nights we've spent sitting on that bench come back me, flooding my senses with the same calm I feel in those moments.

"I tried," I tell her. "Robins wouldn't let me."

"I'm glad Ginger was able to get through to you."

I don't know why, but her admission hits me square in the chest.

Camila didn't invite me here and there's no way she *wants* me, regardless of our truce. But my heart seems to disagree with my brain as it skips a beat in my chest.

Stop it, Jason, I think to myself. *This isn't right.*

This isn't the woman my heart is supposed to be beating for. It's not right.

We watch the people around us as they dance and sing and enjoy life in all the ways I never have.

I'm not nearly as much of a workaholic as Graham is, but that doesn't mean I've indulged in activities outside of school and the hospital. The only time I go to the bar is when I need to relieve some stress and it's rare I drink when I do go. Instead, I help wipe down tables or sweep.

Sebastian, the owner, has no problem with the extra help without having to pay for my labor. He opened the bar a few years ago after travelling here from Italy. As far as I'm aware, his business is about as successful as a surfboard shop in the winter. This is probably due to his decision to hire Graham, though.

Either way, I rarely ever go to the bar to actually drink. Going out and letting loose isn't something I have craved before. I like being in control.

But now, as I stand here watching my colleagues and the residents of the village enjoy the beautiful weather and crafted instruments, I find myself turning to the woman at my side.

She's not the woman who will be at my side in a few months. That woman has long hair and dresses in sweatsuits when she's not working. That's the woman that should be on my mind right now.

"Hey," Paxton says as he comes to stand beside us and puts an arm around Camila's shoulder. "It's pretty cool, isn't it?"

"I'm starting to get what you were saying," Camila admits.

"See? You should always trust my judgement."

She shrugs out of his hold, essentially warning him about his narcissism, but he only chuckles and starts messing with the camera in his hands.

"I have to head back to the site. Are you coming?"

Something in me twists and tightens as I wait to hear Camila say, "Yes." The last thing she wants to do is stand here next to me in this heat, truce or no truce. Hell, even I find myself to be miserable company at times.

But my head snaps towards her when she answers, "No," instead. "I think I'm going to hang out here for a little bit."

Paxton eyes her skeptically, then glances at me over her head. "You aren't going to get mad at me later for leaving you?"

Camila scoffs. "You act like I'm always rude to you."

"You are." She turns to face him, maybe swing her raised fist at him, but he's quick to back up a few steps. "But you are also an amazing little sister."

"Uh—huh."

"Can you get her back to the site later, Jay?"

I nod, ignoring Camila's curious stare, and bounce on the heels of my feet.

"Thanks." With that he scampers off towards Liam and one of the cruisers.

"Do you hold grudges often?" I ask the woman beside me as I watch the dancers in front of us.

She turns her attention towards me. "Only when necessary."

Against my better judgement, I crack a smile. I've been doing a lot of things against my better judgement lately and each decision stems from the same person.

Camila starts to sway to the music as her fingertips tap against her thigh to the beat. A few of my colleagues have joined the dancers and are doing a horrible job at matching the rhythm. Curiosity makes me itch in seeing what the woman beside me is capable of.

Maybe it's the truce we made or some hypnotic beat to the music, but I find myself staring down at Camila and asking, "Do you want to dance?"

Chapter Thirteen

CAMILA

I think I may have lost my mind. That or I'm dehydrated and about to pass out. Either way, there is no plausible explanation for why Doc is staring at me with those brown eyes that remind me of melted chocolate and asking if I want to dance. Nor is there a reason as to why my fingers itch to accept the metaphorical hand he has stretched out to me.

Me. The same woman he barely tolerated a little over a week ago.

"I'm sorry," I say, "I think I heard you wrong. It sounded like you asked me to dance."

"I did."

Okay, so the verdict is I'm crazy.

He rubs at the back of his neck. "We don't have to if you don't want to, I just—"

"I do."

What the hell, Camila?

Not even two days ago, I told Paxton the last thing he has to worry about is me falling for Doc, and here I am: jumping at the opportunity to dance with him.

But it's just one dance and it's not one that involves touching. It's just a polite activity between friends because we called a truce. The truce is why I'm nodding my agreement.

It's fine.

Trying to lighten the nerves now swirling through me, I joke, "If you think you can keep up."

He tilts his head with a smirk. "I promise not step on your toes."

"That's not the kind of dance their doing, Doc." I point out.

"You're going to have to teach me. I'm only used to ballroom dancing with all of the galas and charity events my mother hosts. And it's Jason."

The mention sends my mind back to a memory with Ben. He used to go to a bunch of black-tie events for movies. Ones I could never go to.

That spot was strictly reserved for the woman he held on display, not the woman he hid in the shadows.

"It's not as luxurious as it sounds," he told me when I asked what they were like.

He ran a finger down my arm as my naked body laid on top of his on the bed of my pull-out couch.

"Says the man who goes to an abundance of them." I poked his chest playfully. "You don't get to be bored while the rest of us are on the sidelines."

"Bored, huh?" His hand left my arm and travelled a seductive path to my sheet covered ass. He squeezed, pulling me closer.

I couldn't help the blush that crept up my skin at his touch. He always knew how to make me speechless. "I'm serious," I shoved at his chest, but he didn't so much as budge.

His smile grew. "I am too."

Through a giggle, "Ben! Tell me what they are like."

He settled onto his back, releasing his hold on me. I laid my head on his chest, watching him ponder. "There's lots of people. People from all around the world." He moved his hands as he spoke as if he were painting the picture in front of me. "The food is the size of my palm, but they're so addicting that you end up eating twenty of them by the end of the night."

I laughed as I imagined Ben scoffing down a tray of snacks. "What about the music? Is there dancing?"

At that, he started to caress my skin again with one hand, while the other played with my long, black hair. "Yes."

The image of Ben dancing with his arms around another woman—a woman I could picture perfectly—made me regret ever asking.

"But I don't dance."

"Why not?"

He sat up, pulling me with him so we were both sitting on the creaky mattress, the sheet falling from my chest. He leaned his face close to mine, his lips barely a whisper away. "I never have the right dance partner."

Then, his lips crashed to mine and I envisioned him whisking me away at one of the galas.

Now, as I watch these lively people dance and enjoy the rhythm of their hearts, I couldn't care less about galas and ballroom dancing.

"Well," I tell Doc as I lead him towards the center of the circle. "We're going to have to rectify that."

He follows me. I start to mimic the way others are dancing, swaying my hips with my hands out to the side.

I'm not nearly as good as the rest of them, but I'm a lot better than my partner.

His moves are stiff, and his hands are still locked at his sides.

"You might want to loosen up a little," I tell him.

He frowns at me and it's the cutest thing I've ever witnessed. Well, since his nose wiggling the other day when I accidentally hit him.

I laugh and step closer.

"Here," I place a hand on his hip, trying my best to ignore the sensation tingling from his skin to mine, and guide him, "like this."

We get lost in the movements. My hands try to guide his body out of the box he's dancing in and into the circle he's supposed to be moving to, while he cracks jokes and grumbles, causing me to laugh so hard my belly aches.

The dancers move in circles around us with their skill and the music lights up the mood. It's a complete contrast to the dark and sweaty clubs Lily and I have been to. Those are full of shameless moments and forgotten secrets. You go in looking hot and come out drenched in sweat with ringing in your ears and the endorphins quickly wearing off.

Here, there are no strobe lights, and the only heat is from the sun.

It's refreshing. Doing this. With him.

And that thought, scary enough, doesn't scare me as much as it should.

Casually, I pull from his touch and straighten.

"You're a natural, Doc," I joke in hopes of dissipating the fire burning inside me.

To my disappointment, the distance only seems to make my skin itch from the loss of his touch.

Shit. Shit. Shit.

CHAPTER FOURTEEN

CAMILA

"Am I going to regret leaving you at the camp?" Paxton asks from behind me as I fix the blanket on my cot.

"Why?"

"I don't know. Maybe because you're here to work on yourself and yet you were grinding on Jason last night."

I nearly vomit from his words. "Please never use the word 'grinding' again."

"What else would you call what you two were doing?"

"Dancing, Pax. We were dancing." I turn to face him, before reaching behind him for my bag. "Along with a handful of other people, I might add. And how would you even know when you left?"

"I have eyes everywhere, Camelot. All I'm saying is you two seemed pretty comfortable with each other."

"We're friends." The words fall from my lips before I have time to catch them, but they don't feel like a lie.

We're friends. Doc and I are friends.

The thought sends warmth to my chest.

"Friends don't touch each other like that, Camelot."

My mind floods with memories of last night. Doc's laughter cascading down my spine like the sun warms my skin on a hot day.

His fingers delicately holding my shoulders as I guided him. He didn't hold me like I was made of porcelain. He held me like he was scared if he gripped too hard, I'd become dangerous. He held me like I'm a live wire.

And I don't know why, but it only made me lean into his touch more.

But that's normal. *Right?*

"Can we please stop talking about this?" I plead as we both leave the hut and walk along the path.

"You think I like talking about my little sister and her dating life? I almost lost my lunch five times just watching you yesterday." He fake gags.

I hit him in the stomach with my arm, which only makes him grin devilishly. "You're annoying."

"Aw," he wraps an arm around my shoulder, pulling me into his side. "You missed me. Just admit it."

"If anyone missed anyone, it's you who missed me. Aren't you the one who begged and begged for me to fly here?"

"Aren't you the one who was miserable for months without me? You called me nonstop saying 'Paxton, I miss you.'" He mimics my voice. "'When will you be home, Pax?'"

"I think your memory is broken."

He shakes his head with a smile. "You know, if you keep this up, I'm not sure anyone will be willing to drive you into town today."

This is the reason Paxton is travelling to a different site without me today. I need to go into town and call Kyra to see if she has new leads for me.

My hope is to catch one of the members here to hitch ride before they all drive away. Apparently scheduling is neither my brother's nor my forte.

"I hope she has something for you, Camelot," Paxton tells me as he squeezes me closer.

I smile back because I'm supposed to. Because it's what is expected. I'm supposed to want to have a job to come back to, right?

But something hollows out inside me at the thought of having to leave this place.

Paxton lets me go when we reach the community building. He kisses my cheek and turns on his heel in the other direction towards Liam. I search the last three vehicles parked outside.

I step closer to them, standing on my tiptoes to try and see around them to find any of the drivers. When I come up short and decide to sit on the bench to wait, I hear a familiar voice behind me.

"Are you planning on hot wiring one of them?"

Ja—Doc appears behind me with a small smirk on his lips. I bite back the grin on my own and swallow the excitement blooming inside me.

What is wrong with me?

"Depends," I start, "how quickly do you think I can make it before getting caught?"

"In this region? Oh, a solid twenty miles if you're careful."

I nod, thoughtfully, before we both release a small chuckle at our joke. "Any chance you're heading into town?"

He passes me to toss a bag in the car. "Do you need a ride?"

"How kind of you to offer," I say before jumping into the passenger seat.

The driver's door opens as Doc climbs in. "I was worried I'd have to get on my knees and start begging you," he jokes.

I'm grinning from ear to ear. "I would never make you kneel." A pause and then, "Well, not without witnesses."

He shakes his head and laughs before reversing out of the spot and taking us into town.

"I'm sorry, Camila," Kyra utters through the phone with sincerity. "I know you've been work'n hard and are wait'n for your big break."

"No worries," I twist the phone cord around my finger. "There will be one down the line."

"That's true. I'm glad you're look'n at this from the positive side."

Am I?

My tone is cheerier than it should be, or I intend for, but that doesn't mean I'm not upset I don't have a job. I have enough saved to pay my bills for the next two or three months, but after that?

The last scene I shot was for the movie with Ben. It filled in for one of the lesser seen characters. The memory is still fresh in my mind as if it were yesterday.

My breaths came out ragged as I yanked the hair of the woman standing across from me. I tried to be gentle. This was fake, after all, but it's hard to have a gentle fight.

She threw a punch towards me. I dodged. She bent. I kneed her. This process continued until she crouched on top of my body with an arm ready to swing, and the director yelled, "Cut!"

Instantly, the woman—I think her name was Melanie—smiled. She stood and held a hand out to me to which I took. There was a small scrape on the side of her face from my nails, but it's nothing a little makeup couldn't fix.

"Good work." She patted my back. "You had some new moves in there."

"I had to make some adjustments with your moves." I smiled through the sentence.

She walked to the other end where she had someone fixing her hair and makeup. I rolled my shoulders, about to make my way to my station, when my eyes landed on him.

Ben stood in the shadows with his arms crossed over his chest, and his body turned towards me, but all of his attention was on the woman at his side.

He could have watched me during the scene and no one would have batted an eye. He would just be watching the show. But Ben considered it too risky so he never so much as made eye contact with me for more than five seconds before all of his attention disappeared.

I understood back then. Now, I want to kick myself for being so foolish.

The door to the store opens, bringing me back to the present as Doc steps inside. When his eyes catch mine, I smile at him. He nods, but doesn't look away.

Suddenly all of the doubts and stresses seem to ease off my back long enough for me to tell Kyra bye and hang up the phone.

I debate calling Lily too. I haven't spoken to her since I arrived, and she normally reaches out to me daily. The thought of having to put up a front again makes the idea dissipate.

By the time the phone is plucked back into its spot, Doc is in front of me.

"Are you," my words come out scratchy, so I clear my throat and try again. "Are you making a call?"

"Yeah. I'll just be a second."

Something flickers in his expression. If I was good at reading people, I'd say it was sadness or dread.

Who could he be calling that would make him this torn up over it?

I want to ask more questions, but he reaches for the phone before I have a chance. So I go outside to wait in the car and give him the privacy he gave me.

CHAPTER FIFTEEN

JASON

"You owe me," Graham said on the other end of the line during our phone call earlier. "There's only so much one guy can take."

"Ignore him," Piper, Graham's girlfriend, broke in. "We've got everything handled, Jason."

I let out a long sigh. It's not their responsibility to pack up my things for me, but here they are. I'm sure Hazel's probably there too. And Jasmine…

God, I'm an ass.

"Thank you, guys," I mumbled.

"Oh my—someone call a doctor." Graham exaggerated. "I think I'm going to have a heart attack. Jay just said…*thank you*."

Twenty-seven years old and he's still cracking jokes.

A few female laughs came from his end and my chest seems to ache. I'd never say it out loud, but I miss them.

Each and every one of them.

"I can't complain though," Graham continued. "Jaz is getting the worse end of the stick out of all this. I'll finally be able to have all those karaoke nights you don't let me have."

"You do that anyway."

"Yeah, but now it won't be accompanied by your grumbling and taking the remote."

He joked. It's what he does best. But I could hear the underlying sadness in his tone. Just like I'll never admit I miss them, Graham will never admit he doesn't want me to move.

This is all a long time coming, though. I'm almost twenty-eight years old with no family of my own. I'm not the romantic type like Graham, but I do want a family.

A big one.

So as much as my heart is screaming "no", my head is doing every logical thing it can to reach my destination.

"I can feel your thinking like a bus hit me," Camila says from the passenger seat, pulling me out of my thoughts.

We left the general store about six minutes ago and neither of us have said a peep since. Hints the whirlwind of thoughts replaying in my mind.

"I'm not asking you to divulge in your many, many secrets, but maybe think a little less?"

My mouth quirks at her humor as I adjust my grip on the steering wheel. "Sorry. Just have a lot on my mind."

"Yeah." She lightly pats her thighs with her hands. "I got that."

We fall into another moment of silence. This is usually where I'm most comfortable. It's one of the most difficult things to have to come up with small talk or more than a one-word answer.

I never quite understood why others felt the need to fill an empty space.

Yet, as I sit in this enclosed space with Camila, her floral perfume wafting to my nose, there is this burning desire to say something.

It's not out of anxiety or awkwardness, but just because I want to hear more from her. *About* her.

I hate myself for it.

Luckily, she beats me to it with, "How long are you staying here?"

I peek a glance in her direction, surprised at how simple the question is. Simple and yet causing a riot in my stomach. "About two weeks."

"Me too," she exclaims. Then, she softens her tone and asks, "Do you think it's strange that I'm kind of dreading it?"

"That you have two more weeks?"

"That I'm leaving." She's quiet for a moment, staring out of the plastic window I put up.

Her hair is too short to stay pinned so it flies in the wind as we drive and blows into her face.

"It's funny, you know? I almost booked a plane flight back to the city the second I got here and met you— no offense."

"None taken."

"But now…I don't know. When I get back, there will be bills to pay and no job to pay them with. There will be responsibilities I'm not ready to face again. Not yet."

I take in her words, reading between the lines. It doesn't slip my notice that she hasn't used the word "home" once.

"It's stupid, I know." She waves her hand dismissively.

"It's not. I have…responsibilities of my own I'm not ready to return to either." Not ready to even say aloud apparently.

God, I'm such a mess.

Wretched: unpleasant or of poor quality.

"We're a mess, huh," Camila takes the words right out of my mouth.

"At least you're a beautiful mess."

Shit.

Shit.

Shit.

That was meant to be a joke. Something to lighten the mood. But the second it left my lips—

Shit.

What the hell, Jason?

"Did you just compliment me, Doc?"

I keep my gaze trained on the road, swallowing hard. A blush creeps across my skin.

"I didn't know you knew how to flirt."

Flirt?

Flirt: behave as though attracted to or trying to attract someone.

That's not what I'm doing. Is it?

Shit.

There are hundreds of words in the English language and yet that is the only one swirling in my mind right now.

"Listen, Camila, I—"

"Relax, Doc."

"Jason."

"I get it. You didn't mean it that way."

My brain commands my head to nod, agree with her statement, but my body knows it's a lie.

Why is it a lie?

I'm…I can't be flirting with Camila. I can't find her attractive.

Not after what I did before I got on the plane to come here. The excited shrieks and the pop of champagne bottles still rings in my ears.

I can't pursue Camila. Especially since she is here to work on herself. To get over a relationship with a guy who cheated on her.

These reminders play on repeat in my mind, etching them into my skull, but it won't set in. No matter how hard my brain presses the chisel to the bone, the words won't stay. The warnings vanish.

What scares me the most is that I settle back into my seat without agreeing to her statement, as my fingers seem to twitch in an odd urge to reach for the hand she

117

has propped on the top of the water bottle only a few
inches from mine.

CHAPTER SIXTEEN

CAMILA

The heat of the campfire bites at my skin, warming me from head to toe. It sizzles and pops as the smoke bellows into the star-filled sky.

It's been three days since I went into town and found out I have no job waiting for me. Three days since Ja—Doc called me beautiful. Although, I'm sure that was more of a mistake than it was intentional.

The look of panic on his face is still burned in my mind. Who knew it would be so detrimental to compliment me?

He only called me beautiful. Any one can be beautiful. It's not like he said I'm cute or sexy.

I nearly laugh at the thought. Saying I'm sexy would mean he finds me attractive, and, with how he responded to just beautiful, that's far from what he feels when he looks at me.

Now, we all sit around a fire as Paxton and Liam tell stories of the things they saw on previous trips. Some of the things they divulge are almost too wild to be believable.

I listen to their stories, laughing and smiling at all the right moments, but my mind is elsewhere tonight.

In less than two weeks, I will be on a plane to go back to the city. A city that will contain no prospects for me, but my cold, lonely studio apartment.

To top it all off, the man who's been the only distraction from reality, will also be on the same plane ride. Turns out, he lives in the same city.

Although, he didn't seem very thrilled about the fact that we live in the same area. If I didn't know any better, I'd say he dreaded the idea of bumping into me outside of this camp.

It would be another lie to say it didn't make my heart sink inside my chest when I suggested us staying in touch and all he said in return was, "I usually have long shifts at the hospital."

He's not interested in me, I get it. But can't we still be friends?

Or has he only been nice to me because he feels compelled to?

If I find out Paxton had anything to do with the way Doc's been treating me, I wi—

The sound of female laughter interrupts my thoughts. I turn my head to find the man of my thoughts standing off to the side of the campfire, tucked in the shadows, with Sam hanging on his arm.

She's playfully swatting his bicep as she leans her head back in laughter.

My grip on the beer bottle tightens as something twists in my gut.

There's no valid explanation for the way I'm feeling as I watch them, but it's there. All of it. And it churns even more when his gaze meets mine.

I smile, small, but hopeful.

His mouth doesn't so much as twitch before he brings his own beer to his lips, his eyes never leaving mine.

Sam continues to mumble things to him, but he doesn't say a word back. He doesn't even look at her.

Does she feel the same tingling sensation I do when I touch him?

All of his attention is on me as it slowly skates down my body.

Suddenly hot from the fire—definitely the fire— my fingers graze along my collarbone in an attempt to adjust the collar of my shirt.

He tracks the movement.

I slide the same hand back down my stomach to tug my shirt down over the stretch of exposed skin from the way I'm lounging in the chair.

Doc watches.

All of these actions are done by me, but his intense stare makes every touch feel new. Every touch burns. It almost feels like, even though he's a long stretch from me, he's right beside me holding my hand.

It's this thought, this craving, that makes me stand and stride over to him. I stop beside Sam, drawing both of their attention towards me.

"Hey, Camila," she says. "I haven't seen you around much lately."

"I've been a bit of everywhere." *Except for the medical building. That place I've been avoiding like the plague.*

"How's your arm, by the way?"

She's referring to yesterday morning when I may or may not have been watching where I was going and knocked my arm against a brick wall.

Dr. Robins happened to be a witness and said there may be internal bruising, but nothing serious. If the ache every time I move it a certain way is anything to go by, there's definitely some bruising.

Nothing major though.

Except Doc is staring at me so intently like Sam told him I fell from a cliff.

Staring at him, but answering Sam, I say, "It's nothing serious. Just a bruise."

Doc nods fractionally, but I watch his eyes trail to the arm in question and suddenly it burns for an entirely different reason.

"Why are you out here and not with the rest of the group by the fire?"

It's a question for Doc, but Sam is the one who answers. "Jason isn't a fan of people. You'd be lucky to get three words out of him."

This makes me tilt my head in confusion. He's had no problem talking to me.

Yeah, he hasn't told his whole life story, but I haven't told him mine either. He's been nothing but friendly and open since the day we called our truce.

Hell, even when I was yelling at him about the snake bite, he didn't lash out or groan once. He simply helped me and went about his day.

Now that I think about it, though, there's been more than one instance of comments like Sam's.

Everyone's curious looks when Doc sat down beside me in the dining hall. The "what do you have on him?" question more than one person has asked me when Doc starts a conversation with me first.

Or, most recently, the startled confusion etched into everyone's expression when Doc laughs or smiles.

I open my mouth, about to ask Sam if I can speak to Doc alone, when someone else shoos her away. She's barely walked three feet from us before I advance on the man swarming in my mind.

"Why does everyone seem so afraid of you?"

He takes a sip of his beer, his stare leaving me. "You're not."

"I'm different."

"Yeah," he releases what sounds like a mix of a sigh and a laugh. "You are."

This man is more of a puzzle than those riddles Lily sends me on occasion.

"I should get to bed." He turns to leave. "Good night, Camila."

Camila. Not Bell.

I don't know why, but it makes my chest ache. It feels impersonal and like he's taking two steps back from all the progress we made.

I grab his arm, stopping him from leaving. "Why do you turn hot and cold so much?"

He doesn't look at me. Just picks at the bottle in his hand.

"I don't get it. One second, you're being all sweet and normal—although according to everyone else, it's not normal for you—and the next, you're giving me the cold shoulder."

"I really should get to bed."

"Did I do something wrong?"

"Just let me go, Camila. *Please.*"

Instead of doing just that, my fingers dig into his skin firmer as I weigh my options. Then, after realizing we're still near a group of people, I lace his fingers with mine and drag him away.

"What are you doing?" he hisses.

I don't answer until we're tucked into shadows in the same place we've met countless times before. The same place we called a truce. Except, the bench is closer to us now and neither of us choose to sit.

"Camil—"

"No," I spin to face him. "We're in the safe—truce place now. So…tell me," I softly plead.

Really, he doesn't owe me anything outside of our pleasantries. We never decided we were friends, and we definitely aren't anything more than that. We can't be.

But every time I'm around him, there's this strange pull between us, an electric charge, that makes my brain fuzzy and my chest warm.

And every time we touch…it's like a shot of courage straight to my core.

Maybe it's because of the times I've told him the darkest things lurking in my mind or because of all those times Ben hid his true feelings from me for so long, but I want Doc to open up to me.

I want him to feel as comfortable with me as I do with him. Even though everything inside me is saying this is a bad idea.

Especially because Doc doesn't so much as meet my gaze as he fiddles with that damn ring finger again. We aren't friends and I…

"I thought…" I trail off, not knowing how to voice the thoughts in my mind. "God, this is crazy."

"What's crazy?" He finally looks at me.

"This," I gesture between us. He narrows his eyes at me. "I mean, not us, but—I guess I thought we were becoming friends but obviously that assumption is wrong."

"We are friends," he mumbles so quickly as if it hurt him for me to think otherwise.

Scoffing, "Really? Then why am I the only one who's been sharing their whole life story."

"You didn't share your whole life story, Camila. All you told me were—"

"The things I can't even tell my best friend," I nearly scream.

He flinches at my words, but keeps his eyes locked on mine.

This is all so fucking frustrating. Here's this guy I barely know, who saved my life, is kind to me and apparently not anyone else, and is so easy to talk to that I told him things I can't even admit to the people I love.

A man who makes me feel alive from just being near me.

Yet, he couldn't care less about that fact.

Ben, at least, would lie to me.

I'm so stuck in my head and boiling with confusion that I don't realize Doc's moved until my hand is gently held in his and he's tracing lines on the back of my hand.

"I'm not great at the whole people thing," he tells me.

"Yeah, I picked up on that."

"But there's…*something* about you that just…"

My body turns towards him completely, tuning into the words he's not saying. The words I hope he finds the courage to admit, even if *I'm* not ready to hear them.

"Then, you feel it too? This weird pull between us." I'm laughing off the seriousness as I ask the question.

He is a doctor so maybe he will have a diagnosis for the turmoil inside me. Maybe I'm just sick.

He adjusts our hands so his fingers are laced through mine and I realize I never pulled away. He squeezes once as if to say "yes" in the only way he knows how.

"It's not from the snake bite?" I joke. I *hope*.

Doc drops his gaze to our interlocked hands as his thumb traces tantalizing circles on my skin. He stares at the spot, memorizing the feel.

My heart nearly beats out of my chest at his proximity and the fire igniting inside me.

"I'm so confused," I admit.

He lets out a small, disbelieving scoff. "You're not the only one."

Ignoring the flutter in my chest, I blow out an exasperated breath. "You never answered my question."

"I..."

The pause between his next words makes everything in me freeze. When he sighs and drops his head to stare at his feet, the organ in my chest seems to step closer to the bars around it, just to get a glimpse at the man torn in front of me.

Suddenly, it's as if every emotion has come flooding back as I realize I'm tucked in the shadows with another man who sets my skin aflame, and a memory of Ben comes back to me.

He would drag me into a storage closet in the hall when no one was looking, locking the door, and muffling my giggles with a kiss.

"You have no idea how hard it was to stay away from you," he told me when we finally broke apart. His words were barely above a whisper; I was surprised I could hear them over my racing heart.

"You seemed perfectly content away from me." I played with the zipper of his hoodie.

Ben's arms tightened around my waist. "You just missed all of the times I was staring at you."

His statement should have sent the butterflies through me that it usually did, but that time, all I could think about was how much I wish I *knew* he stared at me. He wasn't allowed to and there was no one I could ask.

"Why…" I started, my voice wobbly as I spoke. "Why do we have to keep hiding?"

His hold loosened on me. "We talked about this, Cami. I—"

"You're engaged. I know."

My eyes couldn't meet his. It was too hard to look in those blue pools of his and see the impatience and annoyance I always found when I asked such questions.

"But what about me?" I wanted to ask. "You said you were ending it, but something always gets in the way and I'm left here in the shadows." All of the words were on the tip of my tongue, but I couldn't force them out.

Instead, it felt as if the walls of the closet were caving in around us.

Ben's fingers found my chin, dragging my gaze up to his. "Don't do that. You make it sound like I'm the bad guy. You know you are the one I want, Cami."

"But what about her?" I wanted to ask. If I'm the one, why do I feel more like the second woman than the princess in the fairy tales?

"After this movie is over, we won't have to keep doing those promotions and the engagement will be done. It's all for publicity, you know that."

Back then, I nodded my head and let him kiss all of the doubts away. If it were Ben with me now, he would have already consumed me with his touch.

But, unlike Ben, Doc seems just as confused and unsure as I do.

In fact, he's barely touched me at all.

The same insecurities that haunted me during and after Ben suddenly come back to me. They scream in my mind and etch their violent words into my skull.

You aren't good enough.

You're only worth of what your body gives.

I close my eyes and internally plead for the voices to shut up. To leave me alone. But each one lashes at me like a whip.

You will always be the secret tucked in the shadows.

No one wants to be seen with you.

You aren't e—

Something falls over my shoulders, pulling me from my thoughts and dispelling all of the memories. I open my eyes to find Doc standing in front of me and adjusting his jacket around my shoulders.

"What are you doing?" I ask, frozen in place.

His hands rest at the collar of the jacket, and I wonder if it's to hold me still. "You look cold."

"Oh…"

"Did you know that hugs are known to release oxytocin which calms your nervous system and lifts your mood?"

Chirping crickets echo around his words, the only background music to this private moment.

"They help reduce blood pressure and inflammation, ultimately being a good medicine for the heart." Doc hasn't let go of the jacket, nor has he backed up even an inch from me.

"Why are you telling me this?"

"Because…I wanted you to know the reasoning behind what I'm about to do."

"What—?"

He lets go of the jacket and gently wrap his arms around my back. He keeps his hands in safe, decent positions, but it doesn't matter. His touch still sends a current of heat strong enough to melt the tension inside me.

As if his touch has flipped a switch inside me, I lower my hands to wrap around his waist and grip the back of his shirt as I lean into him. The scent of smoke and lemon is etched into his clothing.

When his arms tighten around my body and his nose nuzzles in my hair, I feel like I've been shot to the moon.

"I shouldn't be doing this," he whispers.

Those words are what I expect to be a warning before he pushes away or pulls me further into the darkness. It's what Ben always did, and I wouldn't blame Doc for regretting this decision.

Instead of doing just that, Doc holds me impossibly closer and whispers so softly in my ear, "Do you want to go to town with me tomorrow?"

It's such a simple and innocent request that I find myself doing the exact opposite of what I promised.

Not wanting the bubble around us to pop, soaking up all of the newfound energy and courage his touch brings me, and nod into his chest.

CHAPTER SEVENTEEN

JASON

Date: a social or romantic appointment.

Emphasis on social.

The plans I made with Camila for today are for a *social* outing. Not anything romantic.

And I'm simply deprived of all social contact. This is why I'm bustling around today with a grin on my face—or so everyone has pointed out.

It's not a date. It *can't* be a date.

Not when there is only a week and half left until I am supposed to be on a plane to return to the city.

I sit down on the bench outside of the community building. This is where Camila and I agreed to meet after I begrudgingly let her go last night.

There's much to do in this region, but Paxton mentioned a nearby beach during one of his stories. Luckily, I managed to bribe Johnson for the car he reserved today.

My leg bounces beneath me as I check my watch for the time. Yep, same time it was twenty seconds ago.

Why am I this nervous?

It's not a date and friends don't get nervous about seeing each other. Except, friend feels like a lie when it comes to Camila.

It doesn't nearly hold as much weight as it should.

"Missing me?"

I look up from my clasped hands to find the woman running rampant in my mind standing few feet in front of me.

She's wearing a cream-colored dress with a purple lilac design. It's simple and modern, but makes her tan skin radiate against it.

Her hair is down and not the matted sweaty mess it usually is, although it's still beautiful that way too. I like it best when it's a mess because it shows a real part of her.

I'm at a loss for words as she shyly clasps her hands behind her back, putting the outfit on full display for me. Her feet are still wearing those sneakers she's been in for the whole month, but it only makes me love the look more.

"You look beautiful." I shouldn't say it, but I do, because there's no way in hell someone as breathtaking as she is, isn't going to receive a compliment from me.

"You clean up pretty nice, yourself." She steps closer. "Nice to know you own something other than scrubs."

I changed into a pair of shorts and a button up before coming to meet her. Nothing fancy, just a simple going out outfit. It's the same thing I'd wear if I were out with friends.

Definitely.

"So where are you taking me?"

I lead her to one of the vehicles, opening the passenger door for her. "I heard there's a beach nearby. I thought you might like to check it out."

"Sounds like the perfect first date."

I slowly close her door as her words sink in. The plastic cover for the vehicle is off so I'm able to rest my arms on the top of the door as I meet her gaze.

If we're going to do this, I need to be honest. "This isn't a date, Camila. I just want to be clear that this can't be anything more than two friends going out on the town."

Her expression doesn't deflate, nor does she stomp out of the vehicle with curses leaving her lips. Instead, she squeezes my forearm with one of her hands and says, "Friends can go on dates, Doc. I promise I'm not expecting you to get down on one knee."

The mention of marriage makes my stomach churn. One and half weeks. That's it.

I have that sliver of time to reign in all of these conflicting emotions and get back on track for the plan. I made a promise to both Mother and Jasmine. While Mother is the least of my worries right now, Jasmine is the last person I want to disappoint.

Not after she's been there for me so many times.

Most recently it had been a gala she and I attended together with Graham and Piper.

I had been hiding in the corner when Graham found me.

"There are hundreds of people—one of which is a beautiful woman with a company of her own who is also your date—and you have your nose stuck in a book. Correction! A dictionary."

Graham's voice was as annoying as a bee buzzing constantly beside your ear. Close enough to irritate the hell out of you, but too far to crush.

"Seriously, Jay. Do you have to be the weird guy?"

I had actually been reading a dissertation, but that wasn't any of his business.

"Where's your girlfriend?" I asked without looking up from my phone.

"She has a name."

"Great. You should call it and find her."

"Is everything okay?" Piper's familiar voice came between us like the perfect mediator. Graham wrapped his arm around her as she cuddled into his side.

It was sickly sweet. I kept my gaze locked on the phone in my hand.

"Jay is refusing to get off his phone."

"He's probably reading something important, Graham."

"Trumpet, I doubt he's reading anything at all. He's probably just looking at po—"

"Will you *please* take your boyfriend elsewhere?" The request was a yearning plea burning on my tongue. "Preferably far away from me."

Piper smiled but nodded. She understood. She doesn't talk much, and we have only known each other for a little under a year now, but she understands exactly how frustrating socializing can be at times.

"Graham," she patted his chest, "will you dance with me?"

In an instant, he got lost in her. "It would be my pleasure."

She giggled as he whisked her away to the dance floor.

The introductions are what I require Graham for, but after the first forty-five minutes, people tend to stay with their familiar groups. Meaning, I can spend the rest of the evening hiding in the shadows. The only guests I need to entertain are my own and, luckily, Graham brought his own date, and Jasmine has always been a social butterfly.

"Jason." And just like that, the silence disappeared once again.

"Mother." She wore a thin, green gown, the epitome of class, and stood a foot shorter than me. "You look lovely this evening."

"I'm surprised you could see me with your nose in your phone all evening."

Bite your tongue, Jason.

"I see you brought Jasmine." She stayed beside me as we pretended to watch the people milling around us.

I shoved my phone into my pants pocket, gripping it tightly.

"Yet, you two have been separated from the moment you walked in."

"She has friends among the crowd."

"As should you."

I found Graham and Piper spinning around to the classical music. Leave it to him to make even the dullest parties full of light. I had to give some credit to Graham, I guess. Then again, Piper was the reason he smiled.

"I have friends, Mother. They are mingling."

"They are making a show is what they are doing. I assumed you knew better than to come and cause a scene at one of the biggest galas of the year."

According to her, all of the galas are the biggest of the year. All she is looking for is the big investments from the hospital's sponsors. Regardless of whether or not Graham and Piper are making a display—or anyone for that matter—they will continue to donate because it is only about how they appear in society. It is *always* about their image.

A waiter with a tray of champagne passed by. My fingers itched to grab one of the flutes in an attempt to drown out every stab of Mother's. Instead, I fisted my hands in my pockets and feigned nonchalance. "I assure you I have no intention of making a scene, Mother."

"Oh, I am not worried about *you* making a scene, dear. However, I would much appreciate it if you were to crawl out of the hole you are hiding in and appear with Jasmine for at least a second."

I wanted to roll my eyes at her insistence. She claimed I am the one acting like a child and yet...

"I understand you do not feel drawn towards Jasmine—although why is completely lost to me—but she is to be the perfect woman for you. Attraction comes over time, Jason."

There it was: the real reason she insisted I come. Since we were little, our parents have been pushing us together. Everyone within our social circle expects the two of us to walk hand in hand.

"Mother—" I started, but before I had time to say anything more, Jasmine slid up beside me.

It would have been a lie to say she wasn't beautiful in the blue gown hugging her body and the long braid lying over her shoulder and trailing to her hip. She is beautiful on the inside and out, but beauty has never been enough for me.

"Mrs. Young. A pleasure to see you this evening." Jasmine was all flattery as her dark toned hand reached out to shake Mother's. "I was worried I wouldn't be able to speak with you among the many party guests."

"As was I, Jasmine." Mother's mood instantly perked up. "I was just asking Jason where I could find you."

I scoffed, causing Jasmine to subtly step on my toes. "Well," Jasmine wrapped her hand around my arm. Together, I'm sure we looked like a couple to any wandering eyes. "If you don't mind, I was hoping I could steal Jason away."

"Of course."

Jasmine smiled at Mother and I led her in another direction without a glance back.

"Is there a reason you looked about ready to strangle the woman who gave you life?" She mumbled it through tight lips as she smiled and waved at passing strangers. Ever the picture of perfection, except I doubted there is any actual real flaw to Jasmine.

"Do you need a reason?" I stopped when we reached Graham and Piper. We positioned our hands on one another in the classiest embrace to gently sway to the music.

"She's not that bad." I raised an eyebrow to which she sighed. "Maybe a little bad. Good thing I saved you."

"Good" may have been a bit of a stretch. "Yes, good thing."

"You really are the life of the party. I don't know why your mother and Graham say otherwise." The sarcasm was strong.

"I know. Doesn't get better than this."

"Speaking of Graham. I met his wonderful girlfriend, Piper, and I must say—she is way out of his league."

"Don't worry. I remind him of it every day."

She laughed and shook her head. Her long braid swayed in the process. "Ever the diligent friend, you are."

The music descended into a smoother crescendo with the cello making occasional screeches. Who hired the band, again? Classical music and its fans have always been a mystery to me.

Groaning, I glanced around the room for the closest exit. "Please tell me this party will be over soon."

Jasmine lightly tapped my chest. "Jason, you really know how to make a woman feel special."

"A woman? Yes. You are not just any woman though. You are my future wife according to the paperwork."

"Ah, any chance we can add an addendum to have a summer wedding instead of spring? I have a trip planned in March and the hotel doesn't do refunds."

"Cicadas come out this summer and the wedding hall is packed for the fall. How about we push it to a winter wedding for next year?"

"Oh, shoot! I have two conferences in the winter."

"I have a few the following year. Reschedule for…" I pretended to check my watch as if it will have my made up schedule printed on it. "Five years from now?"

"Perfect!"

If there's anything Jasmine and I agreed on, it's our lack of interest in dating one another, let alone marrying.

Jasmine is a wonderful and a highly successful woman, but she is far from my type. We grew up together and are nothing but friends. Both of us intended to keep it that way.

I scoured the room behind Jasmine's head, searching for an exit. The only one available would force me to pass Mother and Father on the way. I checked the corner of the room where the bar is. It's empty except for a few lone persons waiting for a drink.

"Want a drink?" I asked as I returned my attention to Jasmine.

"Depends. Will it find me in a reasonable time frame?"

"It's astounding how well you know me."

She loosened her hold on me, dropping her arms to her sides. "Go. I want to dance with Graham for a song anyway."

Him and Piper were still swaying off to the side, closer than before. "I don't know he will let you take him from her."

"He has no choice. I never see him anymore and he still owes me a dance from last time."

I chuckled softly, shaking my head at her insistence before we separated. Me to the bar and her to the happy couple at the other end.

Normally, I would have already been gone by now—a distant memory to the party guests, but Mother has been watching me like a hawk since I arrived.

Back then, I thought Jasmine and I were only one of Mother's out-of-reach fantasies.

Now, as I stare at the brown pool of Camila's eyes, lost in the way her hand is still caressing my skin and sending shots of soothing electricity through my veins, I wish that were still true.

I wish I was the kind of man who could keep my promises.

Chapter Eighteen

CAMILA

The beach Doc brings me to is not one you would use as a vacation spot.

It's small, maybe about a mile or two long with a small stretch of the shore before you reach the dark blue water. There is very little sand compared to the mass number of rocks littered around.

It's far from a romantic area or even a place someone would come to swim. Not that I planned either of these things today.

Escaping Paxton before he had a chance to see my dress and make comments I'm not ready to hear was already a task in and of itself. I didn't pack the dress, Lily must have snuck it when I was looking, but the sun seemed to be beating down at the perfect temperature today.

It just felt natural to put on the dress. And a pair of earrings with my hair as tame as possible in this heat. If I had thought to pack more than one type of shoe, I wouldn't be wearing the worn-out sneakers on my feet right now either.

Although, they're kind of symbolic since they are the same ones I wore the day I met Doc.

The memory, though it occurred only weeks ago, feels so distant now.

"How do you know about this place?" I ask as we walk along the shoreline.

Doc peers out at the water with his eyes squinted. "Your brother mentioned it once or twice."

"I didn't think you actually listened to his stories."

He shrugs. "I don't."

Did he ask Paxton about a spot to take me?

No, he couldn't have. He very clearly stated this is not a date.

Or did he only say that because he was worried I didn't want it to be a date?

Do I want it to be a date?

God, Camila, pull yourself together.

Sure, I'm attracted to him, but...

"Is here okay?" He points to a spot on the ground for us to sit.

I nod and run my hands along the back of my dress to sit, but stop midway when he plops his bag—the one he carried all the way from the car—down and pulls a blanket out. It's small, maybe only big enough for one person.

When it's laid flat, he sits on the sand beside it, giving me the blanket to sit on.

I fight the smile on my face as I slowly sink to the ground.

We stay like this for a little while, just existing in the same space. The water is steady in front of us without waves crashing against the shore.

My mind isn't focused on the view, though. It's running a thousand miles a minute about the lack of distance between us.

If either of us were to scoot a hair closer, we'd be touching. Although, the tingling sensation coursing through me makes it seem as if we already are.

What is it about this man that drives me so wild?

Ben made me wild with endorphins and anxiety too, but Doc... There's something electric in him. He gives me this burst of energy just by his proximity.

I clear my throat. "I'm surprised you asked me out."

He arches a brow at me.

"Sorry. Poor choice of words. I mean, that you asked to spend time with me. I honestly thought you still hate me."

"I never hated you, Camila."

"Please, you loved to make me scowl."

He leans back on his hands. "Oh, I still do. It's nice getting you all riled up."

"What about my anger is so appealing to you?"

Doc pauses for a moment, studying me. "It's real."

"And my happiness, isn't?"

"You tell me. If I remember correctly, you told me you are here to get over a breakup. Have you?"

I stay quiet, pondering over his words.

That is the reason I boarded the plane to come here. To finally figure out myself and move on from

Ben—the man who's kept me lying in bed and barely anything.

The guy who now makes me snap when I see a guy leading a girl on. Just like I did to Doc in the dining hall the other day.

When I planned this trip out, it was my every intention to prove my brother wrong. I'm fine. I always have been.

But if I'm being honest, these past few weeks have only made me realize that I've been trying to prove myself right. To have proof that I am fine and not some broken shell of myself over some guy who didn't even care enough to be honest with me.

The day I ended things comes back to me as I stare out at the water.

After catching him with Elizabeth, I stopped responding to his messages and I avoided him any time I saw his shiny blonde hair nearby. It worked for a solid two days until he dragged me into a corner and confronted me.

"Did I do something wrong?" Ben asked me as he ran his fingers down the side of my face.

The images and sounds of adultery flashed in my mind like a phantom. I shoved his hand away. "I don't think we should continue…"

He scoffed. "What are you talking about?"

"This is over, Ben."

He took a step closer, reaching out to me, but I stepped away from his grasp. "Cami, is this about the engagement announcement that went out? That's just for publicity and—"

The rest of his words drowned out as the act he committed two days ago played on repeat in my mind. My lungs collapsed inside of me, making it hard to breathe.

I don't know why I didn't just tell him I saw him. I couldn't. A part of me hoped that I had imagined the whole thing. Maybe it was all one big nightmare. But my leg was still bruised from the cut on my thigh.

It throbbed with every step he took.

"No," I finally said, stern.

His face flashed with confusion, then betrayal. "What the hell, Camila?"

I shook my head, not able to meet the eyes of the man I thought I would end up with. "Don't make this harder than it has to be." *Please,* I begged internally. "We're done, Ben. I wish nothing but the best for you."

I wanted to believe it was a lie, but I knew it wasn't. Despite everything, in that moment, all I wanted was for him to grab my hand, bring me into the light, and kiss me in front of everyone.

It wouldn't matter that he was with Elizabeth. If he took the initiative, I would forgive him.

So, I walked away before he had a chance to. Before he could make me forget every logical thing in my mind and force me back in the shadows with him.

And I've been running away ever since, always keeping the lights on in fear of the dark closing in again. Afraid I'll become that naïve girl again.

Something falls on my dress and I look down to see I'm crying.

Quickly, I swipe at the wetness on my cheeks before Doc has a chance to see.

Unfortunately for me, I'm not fast enough.

He grabs my wrist, halting my actions, and gently bringing my hands back down to my lap.

"I'm sorry," I choke out with a chuckle, "I'm not even sure why I'm crying right now."

"Did you know," he starts with his attention on my hands as he scoops up a pile of sand and slowly drops it into my palm, "that touching your surroundings can help ground you?"

The grains are rough against my skin as I scrape them between my fingers.

"It's one of the tricks to help relieve anxiety."

Then, with so much grace I fear I might break if he's any more delicate, he lifts his hands, after shaking the sand off of them, and wipes the tears away with his thumbs.

"It's okay to cry," he tells me with his hands now cupping the sides of my face, forcing me to meet his gaze.

It's so intense that I worry he's peering into my soul. I want to pull out of his embrace before he has a chance to see the girl curled up in a ball in the recess of my mind. The girl who has written "Someone to hold me" on thousands of paper lanterns before sending them off into a never-ending sky.

I'm afraid if he looks too closely, he'll see that the woman who stands tall with a sword in her hand and a full body of armor is really a front to protect the dreamer inside me.

"Bellona." The name is a whisper brushing against my lips as it leaves his.

"W—what?"

"It's the name of a warrior goddess. She wears a military helmet and carries weapons and a torch."

"Is there a reason you're telling me this? I'm not trying to be rude, but I'm not really sure how it relates to me crying like a child." I fake a laugh through the last part to help dissipate the tension.

He brings my face closer to his. So close I can see the gold flecks in his eyes and the small mole on the side of his nose. So close our lips are barely centimeters apart.

My heart starts to beat like a drum in my chest.

"It's the nickname I gave you, Camila. Bell. Because even then, I could see how much of a warrior you are. Well, more so because of how much you like to *start* wars."

"I thought this was meant to make me feel better," I lightly shove at his chest.

"Now," he smiles softly, "I see that you've really just been fighting a battle you didn't sign up for. And you just keep fighting like you are waiting for the day someone will hold your armor and weapons so you can rest in between battles."

His words dance along my skin, lighting a fire inside the pit of my stomach. He only has his hands on my face, gently cupping my cheeks, but it feels like he has chiseled a window into my chest for the sunlight of his affection to peek through.

The scariest part: despite the closet of curtains I have tucked in a closet somewhere, waiting for this exact moment, my heart steps closer to the window to bask in his warmth.

My lips part involuntarily, and his eyes catch the movement. I lean into his touch, waiting for him to make a move, to plant his mouth on mine and make me forget about the man who now makes me shy away from touch.

Doc moves in a fraction more so his lips graze against mine in the softest kiss. It's so beautifully delicate, I can't help, but whisper, "Ja—"

As if a bucket of cold water were dumped on him, he lets go and pulls away. A breeze envelopes my burning skin as I try to catch my breath.

I want to ask what went wrong. If I did something wrong. Surely he felt it too. But then I remember what he said at the car before we left.

This can't be anything more than two friends going out on the town.

For some unknown reason, he can't do more and I shouldn't be wanting more.

So in hopes of releasing some of the tension, I adjust my position and say, "You can't nickname a nickname."

He peers at me curiously.

"Bell for Bellona."

"Of course there's more rules to your nickname thing." He rolls his eyes, fighting a grin.

I laugh and let his calm and comforting presence do just that. Comfort me.

CHAPTER NINETEEN

JASON

"Jaz, do you ever worry about the future?" I asked the woman across the table from me.

She wore a slim navy dress with her long black hair tied in a tall ponytail. We were eating at an upscale restaurant after Mother informed me she reserved a table for the two of us.

Jasmine signed on a new investor for her company—no surprise Mother found out—and Mother thought it would be nice for me to take her out.

"Is this your way of saying I'm getting old?" She bit the piece of steak off her fork before aiming the silverware at me with narrowed eyes.

"We're going to be turning twenty-eight this year, Jaz."

"That's generally how aging works. What are you trying to get at, Jay?"

I stared at the half-eaten scoop of corn on my plate before setting my silverware down and pushing it away.

Mother's insistence on me marrying Jasmine has always been the one thing I easily shot down. I had no trouble telling her no when it came to that.

Jasmine completely agreed with me on the matter too. We weren't romantically interested in each other and why marry someone you weren't attracted to?

But then I started working in the ER and seeing a lot of families and little kids. I didn't grow up with any siblings, if you don't count having Graham and Jasmine around twenty-four-seven. My parents were happy with having only one child.

As I grew and learned more about the world, I realized how much I want a family. A big one.

And as much as it pains me to admit, Mother was right. The best way to accomplish that is by marrying someone I know I can trust. Someone who has the same values as me.

So without any preparation or ring or even a warning, I met Jasmine's confused expression and asked, "Will you marry me?"

Marriage: the legally or formally recognized union of two people as partners in a personal relationship.

In the city, when I have trouble sleeping, I go for a run. It's one of the only effective ways I find clears my head. Here, though, where the stars are so clear in the sky at night, acting as background dancers to the moon, it settles my mind more to sit and enjoy the scenery I won't have in a week.

One week. That's how much time I have left before I get on the plane and back to reality.

Before I have to leave Camila in the past despite how much it makes my chest ache.

I lean forward, planting my hand in my hands.

I'm such an asshole.

Right when she was most vulnerable, I took advantage of her and nearly kissed her. I brought her somewhere secluded just to have her alone. Not for any bad intentions of making a move on her, but just because I wanted to. I still want to.

Despite how wrong it is and utterly fucked up this entire situation is, the idea of forgetting her and pretending we don't live in the same city kills me.

"Mind if I join you?"

My head snaps up at the voice to find the woman occupying my mind as a vision in front of me. She's wearing Paxton's hoodie again and a pair of shorts. The hood is pulled over her head. It warms me to know she feels comfortable enough around me to not care what she looks like.

When she stands off to the side for a moment, I remember the question she asked and nod.

"Couldn't sleep?" She slides into the spot next to me, the space between us being eaten up by a sudden urge to be closer to her.

I lean back, spreading my legs so one of my knees touches hers and that calming current only she carries flows through me. "Yeah. You?"

"You try sharing a tent with Snorer McGee."

A laugh bubbles out of me. "There's a reason no one shares the tent with him."

"My dad built a makeshift soundproof wall with egg cartons when we were younger to help block out the noise. It lasted about a week until my mom got tired of it and decided to take him to one of those sleep doctors."

"Did it not work out?"

"Oh, it did. For five whole glorious years until he went off to college. Then he stopped keeping up with it and—well, we're back at square one apparently."

The images she creates filter through my mind, but the only thing my brain latches onto is a younger version of her.

Has she always had short hair? Or did she used to grow it out and wear it in a braid or pig tails?

Was she the type who would dress up in princess gowns or costumes, or did she go around in comfortable outfits? My only frame of reference is Jasmine, but her parents always dressed her in the finest outfits.

When I have kids, though, I want them to wear superhero costumes or go around the house in just a t-shirt and diaper. I don't want them to even know how to say the word Prada, let alone know what it is.

"What about you?" Camila breaks into my thoughts. "You haven't told me anything about your personal life."

"What do you want to know?"

She leans back, getting comfortable. "Hmm. We'll start easy. Tell me about your family."

Not sure that's as easy as she thinks it is. "Two parents. Mom is the director of the hospital I work for and Dad is the lead manager of a bank. No siblings."

"I was expecting something more sweet or happy. No offense, but what you described almost sounds bleak."

I laugh for the second time tonight. "You're saying a family of three career driven people isn't exciting?"

"Not in the way you describe it." Camila twists in her spot so her legs are crossed beneath her and she's facing me. "Give me a memory. One of your earliest happy memories."

"I thought we were starting off easy."

"If you can't handle this, Doc, you definitely can't handle the other questions I have loading."

I stop breathing for a moment as I watch her.

Doc.

She almost said my name yesterday and now we're back to Doc.

The moment floods back to me like a slap in the face. I almost kissed her. A woman I have no business flirting with or even being alone with.

"Don't leave me hanging. Earliest memory."

"I'm not getting out of this, am I?"

She shakes her head with a grin.

Combing through my memory, I try to find a moment I can share. A moment earlier enough and happy enough to satisfy her request.

Finding a box somewhere in the tether of my brain, I pluck a memory out of it.

"We live in a condo so I didn't have a yard to play in like other kids," I start as the memory resurfaces in my mind. "Mother was never a fan of dirt to begin with anyway so I think the condo was intentional.

I tried out for baseball in…middle school, I think? It seemed like a great activity to do outside of the various clubs and academic work my mother insisted I be a part of. But there was no one who could take me to and pick me up from practices."

I leave out the part about Mother disapproving and finding it to be a distraction.

"I told my parents it was fine, and I wasn't really interested in the sport anyway. I must not have made a pretty convincing case because a few days later, my father took me to the park with Graham, a friend, so the three of us could play baseball together. Mother showed up a few hours later with my favorite cherry ice cream."

It was one of the few days we were all doing something *I* wanted. This is why it's locked away in my mind where nothing can tarnish it.

"You had me until you said cherry ice cream," Camila jokes as she pretends to gag.

I'm grinning from ear to ear. "Have you ever tried it?"

"Cherries are a topping. Not an ingredient."

"You're really going to limit a fruit's potential."

"When the fruit is cherries, yes. Yes, I am."

We stare at one another for a moment, holding our breaths, before we both break out into laughter.

I never knew how light weight it feels when you're the reason for someone's joy until her. Then again, I didn't know a lot of things until Camila got off the plane.

"So," she starts when we've sobered up. "Did you ever try out for the baseball team in high school or college?"

"No. It was a fever dream. Came and went. By the time I started high school, I got too busy applying to medical schools to even consider doing something outside of it."

"Do you regret it?"

"A little, but not enough to be destroyed over it."

We continue talking about the most random things. Learning things about one another that others don't know.

She tells me about a time her parents took her and Paxton to an amusement park and they all thought they lost her in one of the lines, but she had snuck away to try and steal a corn dog from one of the vendors.

I learn about all of her favorites.

Ice cream: pistachio.

Color: violet.

Genre: thrillers.

Out of all of the things she shares, the one I latch onto is about her wish to attend a black-tie event. She's always wondered what it would be like to dress up in a gown and dance a "fancy dance"—as she calls it.

The thought causes images of us at one of Mother's charity galas to filter through my mind. But that's all a daydream.

We laugh and cry from laughing so hard.

The talks distract us long enough that I don't think twice about her shift in her spot and stretching out across the bench to lay her head on my lap.

I don't stand and put her at a safe distance like I should when her eyes flutter close and she curls closer into me. None of the rational thoughts and shouldn't's come to mind when my own eyes fall shut and we both lose track of time.

CHAPTER TWENTY

CAMILA

I shake my head in an attempt to ease the stiffness in my neck. One of these days sleeping on a cot is going to catch up with me and apparently today is that day.

Paxton must have already left the tent because the sun peeks through my eyelids, making me squeeze my eyes shut tighter and roll further away in hopes of blocking out the light.

I barely slept last night after—

My eyes pop open, then blink rapidly at the sunlight as the memories last night come back to me. When my vision is clear, I find a few women walking by as they whisper to each other, pointing at me and Doc. *Doc.*

Quickly, I look above me to find Doc with his arms crossed and his head tilted forward as he sleeps. His brows are pinched together, and I wonder if it's from a bad dream or from how uncomfortable he must be in that position.

I slept for hours with him as my pillow rather than the wooden bench and yet my own muscles are tight and sore. Whoever thought sleeping on a bench would be comfortable?

Cautiously rolling over to face him completely since the onlookers have disappeared, I take advantage of his peaceful form to study him. His dark lashes are longer than mine, nearly brushing the bottom of his eyelids.

His hair is mussed like he ran his fingers through it at least five times before he fell asleep. And his corded arms are tightly locked around his chest as if he feared touching me in his sleep. I don't know if I should feel complimented or insulted by that fact.

I've fallen asleep beside a man before. Hell, I've fallen asleep *on* a man, but it usually ended with me waking up to find their side of the bed empty and my skin cold.

By men, I mean Ben. He was the first one I ever let that close to me and I swore up and down he'd be the last. In the beginning it was because I thought we'd get married one day. As time passed, I swore for an entirely different reason. Letting someone into your bed opens them up to a vulnerable side of you. A side that grants them with too much access to a lovesick heart.

But as I study Doc's face, worn with sleep and probably tense from how comfortable he wanted me to be, I want to break that promise.

My hand reaches up to caress his face. The tip of my index finger traces the seam of his soft lips in the most feather light touch. A rush of electricity races down my spine, but he must feel it too because his eyes snap open, meeting my gaze and catching me with my hand frozen between us.

We stay like this for a moment, both of us holding our breaths in fear of disrupting the consuming bubble around us. It's almost like we're on a rollercoaster, slowly increasing in height as our stomachs drop and sour in anticipation, before we reach the peak and finally plummet into the endorphins.

It's similar to willingly going into a haunted house because you know it will scare you. You *want* it to scare you because of the excitement.

That's how I feel in this moment, frozen on top of Doc, scared that if I move an inch, he'll pull away from me again. Terrified of how badly my heart aches at the idea of that happening.

"So, this is where you've been?" someone sings.

As if both of us have a rope around our neck and someone pulled, Doc and I scramble away from one another faster than is humanly possible.

When I'm sitting up straight and meet the frown in my brother's gaze, I realize we weren't fast enough.

Swallowing the lump in my throat, I roll my eyes to feign as much nonchalance as possible, despite the erratic beating in my chest. "Don't be so dramatic, Pax."

"Dramatic?" He throws his head back. "How else would I interpret finding my sister on top of Jason fucking Young."

My cheeks redden at his phrasing. Through clenched teeth, I say, "I wasn't on top of him."

"And where do you get off making moves on my sister in broad daylight?" Paxton turns his attention to Doc, who's standing by the bench, as far from me as possible, with the guiltiest expression on his face.

It confuses me. Paxton is only joking. He's all bark and no bite. Not when Doc is not a viable threat to me.

But Doc looks as if he's shaking with nerves. Like he committed a horrendous crime and can't wait for the first chance to book it out of here.

What the hell is going on?

All we did was fall asleep on a bench together. Nothing happened. Sure, I may have drooled a little on his pants, but I didn't maim him. Yet, the way he has his head ducked and his hands clenched at his sides tell an entirely different story.

"Doc…" I start, but he cuts me off before I have a chance.

"I have to go." Without so much as an explanation or waiting for either of us to respond, he saunters off in the other direction.

I watch his retreating form as something pinches in my chest.

There's nothing to be worried about. I'm clearly overthinking the entire thing, but I feel like we have reached the top of the roller coaster, only the locks have set and now we're dangling in the air.

We're frozen and I have no idea how to push us forward. I have no idea *why* I want to push us forward, but I do.

Everything in me is begging me to run after him. Grab his hand and squeeze a reassuring "it's okay" like he did for me.

"Did I say something?" Paxton aims a thumb in the direction of Doc.

I stand, adjusting the hoodie around me, before punching his arm. "You probably scared him shitless, Paxton. Thanks for that."

"Ow." He rubs at the spot my fist connected with. "It was just a joke. And if he can't handle that, then he has no reason pursuing you."

"He's not…" I trail off, not sure how to finish the sentence.

If Paxton had asked me a few weeks ago or even yesterday, I would have easily denied all allegations of Doc having feelings for me.

Now, after our outing and talking nonstop last night and laughing so hard my belly ached, I'm not sure that's the truth anymore. I don't think he's in love with me, but something tells me he's at war with himself about how he feels for me.

There's no way he doesn't feel the electricity that courses through us. I may be obtuse sometimes, but I'm not indifferent. We mean something to each other. I just hope he can figure it out while my guard is still down.

Then again, it's becoming harder and harder to barricade my heart from Doc. I'm afraid he found the key where I threw it all those years ago. Now, all he has to do is turn the lock.

I just wish my heart wasn't gripping the bars of its prison so tightly as it watches. The possibility of freedom hurts more than being isolated.

CHAPTER TWENTY-ONE

JASON

Jasmine laughed hysterically at my question; her head thrown back as she caught the stares of a few other patrons of the restaurant.

"Sorry," she claimed as she sobered up and took a sip of her wine. "Your humor is getting better. You should be a comedian."

I crossed my arms as I stared across the table at her. "It wasn't a joke, Jaz."

Slowly, she set the glass back down and adjusted in her seat. "Is this your way of confessing your feelings for me? I'm flattered, but—"

"I'm not in love with you."

Her eyebrows lifted in mock offense. "You really know how to make a woman feel special, don't you, Jay?"

My molars grounded together as I regretted ever asking the question to begin with. I knew she'd make me spell it out. It's one of the things I both love and hate about her.

Swallowing the knot in my throat, I sat up straighter and said, "Why not?"

She guffawed. "You mean, besides the fact that neither of us are romantically interested in the other?"

"Attraction comes with time."

"Now you're starting to sound like your mother."

A low blow, but a blow nonetheless. "Maybe she has a point." I shrugged.

"Jason, be real with me. Where is this all coming from?"

I combed through the pro and con list I made countless times before this conversation was brought up. Usually, I fought heavily on the con side. But, at that moment, every positive seemed to outweigh the negative.

"I want a family, Jaz." It's one of the few truths I have ever said aloud. "We're both going to be thirty in a few years and I want to start a family before then. We might not be attracted to each other now, or even in the future, but I know you'd make a wonderful mom and I—"

"Oh my—you're serious." Her eyes were wide as she stared at me like a stranger sat across from her.

I nodded.

She pushed her chair back and stood, grabbing her purse from where it hung on the back of the chair.

"Where are you going?"

"Somewhere with sane people because clearly you need to be admitted."

"Jaz," I stood, planning to take it all back. To say it was all one big joke, despite how much it made my stomach twist, but she was already striding away.

Now, I listen to the dial tone of the phone once before hanging it up again. The clerk in the store is sighing from his position behind the counter, judging me for wasting so much time to make one phone call.

One.

But this phone call is a big one. A dooming conversation that could either end with me losing one of my closest friends and potential for a secure future or me losing the future I want. A future I didn't even know was possible until about two weeks ago.

If I don't make this call, it could all disappear in less than a week.

What scares me the most is that if I don't make this phone call and lay everything out there, be honest about how much of a backstabbing ass I've been for the past few weeks, I'll be breaking my promise long before I even have a chance to prove to Jasmine she can trust me.

"Fuck," I grunt as I pick up the phone again and dial the phone number I know by heart.

She picks up on the second ring, probably already prepared to tell me off for calling so many times. "How is it that you are thousands of miles away from Graham, and yet still behave the same?"

Normally I'd say something witty back, but my mind is all muddled right now. My body is still locked in the trance Camila put me in. Being away from her has only made me break out in cold sweats.

God, what is she doing to me?

"Jay?"

"Yeah," my voice comes out rough, so I clear my throat. "I'm here."

"Is everything okay?"

No. Everything is the furthest from okay it can possibly be.

"Did Graham call you about the couch? I promise I'm not going to take it. I don't know why he's so attached to it anyway when you sink to the floor in it the second you sit down. How anyone can…"

Her words drown out as my mind runs a thousand miles a minute. It's not Jasmine's image I see in front of me, but a woman with short dark hair and a smile so genuine it makes the sun's light pale in comparison.

A woman whose touch doesn't scorn me or feel unfamiliar when her fingers graze my arm, but who's hand fits perfectly in mine. Who makes the world shine brighter and a heck of a lot more bearable when we're touching even in the least intimate ways.

Hospitable: friendly or welcoming to strangers or guests.

Friendly: kind and pleasant.

No. Neither of those words correctly describe her and how she makes me feel.

I've scoured through the dictionary countless times after I ran this morning trying to find a word to explain the fire she lights inside me.

It's almost like I have been walking around with an ocean full of tsunamis inside me for as long as I can remember. Around other people, the storm brews heavier and makes me sick and irritable.

But Camila carries this torch with her that she uses to help me see the storm inside isn't really that bad. Then, she lights a fire on the beach and waits out the storm with me.

Except, what I'm coming to find is that there is no storm when she's around.

"You're not listening to a word I'm saying, are you?" Jasmine draws me out of my thoughts. "Is this how it's going to be in the future?"

"No," is all I manage to croak out.

Her tone is so lighthearted on her end, the polar opposite of how shot all of my nerves are right now. "Well, if you don't have anything to say, I have a meeting in about five. So why did you call, Jay?"

Shit. She's about to go into a meeting with a handful of people who expect to see her at her best because that's who Jasmine is: always professional and pristine and perfect.

And here I am planning to ruin it all with one sentence.

My heart drops to the pit of my stomach making me want to vomit. I clench the phone tighter as I say, "It can wait. Good luck."

"Thanks. I'll see you in five days!" She hangs up without waiting for a response from me and I'm glad she does, or she would hear the groan escape me.

Five days. That's how much time I have to come up with a plan. I almost wish I could leave sooner so I could talk to Jasmine in person, then find Camila.

We live in the same city, after all. Apparently, the universe has its own twisted humor.

But booking an earlier flight isn't possible when I'm here for a job. To prove myself. Not to get distracted and rung out about relationships.

Except this feel like a lot more than just a relationship. It's as if I'm stuck between a childhood friendship and the promise of the family I always thought I'd find.

Because that's what Camila's touch feels like to me: a family, a home I crave to come back to everyday.

And in five days: I'll either have the key to the front door or will have the house set aflame.

CHAPTER TWENTY-TWO

CAMILA

"Do you want to tell me what's going on in that ugly head of yours?" Paxton asks as we walk back towards the site from the area he and Liam were photographing today.

Ignoring the insult, I say, "Besides a thousand ways to strangle you in your sleep."

He groans. "I said I'm sorry. How long are you going to hold this over my head?"

"As long as it takes until you get it in that thick skull of yours."

"How was I supposed to know he'd be that sensitive?"

Paxton has been grilling me about this morning nonstop. Each time, I give him the cold shoulder and remind him how much of an ass he was to Doc.

Although, something tells me the way Doc shook with nerves had little to do with Paxton and a lot to do with this internal war inside himself.

I've made it my mission to demand answers from him the next time I see him. I went through all of the back and forth with Ben before and look where it got me?

I like Doc—which became clear when my heart dipped with disappointment at how fast he ran this morning—but I'm not going to go down that avenue without a sure fire guarantee I can trust him. Not again.

"How do you think Maya would feel if I found the two of you on a bench and started threatening her?"

He grins sheepishly before wrapping his arm around my shoulders. "See? That's where we're different, Camelot. I would never let you catch me."

I shove away from him, which only makes him laugh harder. He jogs to catch up with me. When he's in step beside me, the humor seems to die.

"Seriously, though. What's going on between the two of you? I thought you swore off dating."

"I didn't swear off dating. Just...dating men I don't trust."

"And you trust Jason?"

Completely? I don't know.

It's hard to give that part of myself up again and to someone I just met a few weeks ago. It's not logical or rational. If it were Lily in my place, I'd tell her to shut it down and run.

But there's something about Doc that makes all of the doubts and worries seem to fade. His presence, his touch, is like a heated blanket wrapping around me in the middle of a winter storm. And I've been freezing for so long that I didn't realize how starved I was for warmth until he showed up.

"I think I'm starting to," I admit.

"Aw," Paxton moves in front of me to pinch my cheeks. "My little sister has a crush."

I swat his hands away, rubbing at the slight sting they left. "Shut up."

He laughs, unabashedly. "Do you want my honest brotherly opinion on this or one that you want to hear?"

My hands start to sweat at what I know he's going to say. Yet, I still go with, "brotherly opinion."

"Okay." He claps his hands behind his back. "I think you should go for it."

This stops me dead in my tracks. "I thought you were giving me your brotherly opinion, not what I want to hear."

"So you admit you like him?"

I cross my arms.

"What you wanted to hear was me telling you *not* to go for it because that's what you think is right."

"And diving headfirst after being cheated on and betrayed is the right way to go?"

He rolls his eyes and sighs as if I'm being impossible. "Everyone heals differently, Camila. Some are better on their own, spending time getting to know themselves and learning how to be without someone. You already know all of that stuff. No matter what happened during or after Ben, you were still Camila. You still are."

I adjust my arms, tighten my grip, then release it.

"What you needed was someone to show you how to trust again. And I hate to break it to you, Sis, but you've also been in a much better mood with Jason around. It's like he hung the moon or something."

At that, I crack a smile and elbow him. "And here I thought you might actually be wise for once."

"See? That's your problem. You think too much. It makes your brain hurt."

"Asshole."

"You love me."

I do. As irritating and annoying he is, I do. "I'm glad you made me come here, Pax."

"Yeah, yeah. Just remember me on your wedding day."

Weddings and marriage are far from my mind right now. I'm not even sure if Doc feels the same way about me, let alone if he can see me in his future.

But I joke back anyway. "You'll be the maid of honor."

He waves his hands beside his eyes, pretending to tear up. "You're going to make me cry."

"Don't be so dramatic. We're killing daylight and you still have to take me into town so I can call Lily."

At the mention of her name, his smile drops, and he grumbles. "I can't believe you're still friends with her."

"Oh, get over yourself and let's go."

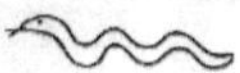

"You sound awfully cheery for someone stranded in the middle of nowhere," Lily comments through the phone pressed to my ear.

I fiddle with the cord, wrapping it around my finger, as I fight the smile on my lips. "I...I think I might have met someone."

She shrieks, nearly piercing my ear drum. I pull the phone away from my ear until I no longer hear the scream.

"Was that necessary?"

"Absolutely! You haven't dated anyone since— well, since before we met apparently. If you don't count the few guys you 'talked' to."

This information is true, considering she doesn't know about Ben. Part of keeping it under wraps is I wasn't allowed to tell anyone about our relationship.

Then, after everything happened, I was too embarrassed to tell Lily the truth. It was hard enough opening up to Paxton when he took me to the hospital.

Now, with Doc—a man I don't have to keep hidden—telling Lily makes me a lot giddier than it probably should.

"Tell me all about him. Is he from there? Or is he one of Paxton's buddies? Please tell me he's Paxton's boss."

"Ewe," the image of Liam with his gray, shaggy hair, and pointed nose comes to mind. "Why would you think it's Pax's boss?"

"Great material for my next book. Brother's best friend is great and all, but brother's boss? The possibilities are endless, Cam."

I laugh at her ridiculousness. I don't have to be with her in person to know she's probably curled up on the floor between her coffee table and couch, with hundreds of sticky notes and half used notebooks littered around her. Her computer is also more than likely propped open in front of her with an unusual Google search on the screen.

"If he's not your brother's boss. Who is he?"

"He's a doctor volunteering here. His name is Jason."

"Not the best name, but that's fine. We can workshop it later."

"Lil."

"Sorry. This is great, though, Hun. I'm so happy for you. When can I meet him?"

This sends something sour in my stomach and makes me even more grateful Paxton stepped outside while I took this call.

Privacy isn't much of his thing, but he saw someone he knew outside and got distracted.

"That's the thing," I start. "He's actually on the same flight as me."

"Why am I sensing a 'but'?"

I fiddle with the cord some more, my fingers getting trapped between the curls. "I don't know. Something just seems off. One minute we are great, and I think we're on the same page, but the next...he's distant." Like he regrets ever touching me to begin with.

"Have you been honest about how you feel?"

That night at the campfire comes back to my mind. I laid myself out there, didn't I? But then he made it very clear we weren't on a date, and I agreed.

"I'm going to take your silence as a 'no'." Lily interjects. "Maybe he's getting mixed signals from you too. You need to lay it all out there, Cam. Then, if he genuinely likes you—and I don't see how he couldn't—he'll make a move."

Her words seem to ricochet inside me. *Lay it all out there.*

It's a solid plan and one I probably should have thought of sooner, but it also means being vulnerable. Not just letting him hold the key to the barricade around my heart but telling him he has it. Showing him how to use it.

That is the scariest part.

Because what if I do that and it all ends the same way it did with Ben? It's hard enough as it is now trying to forget Ben, I don't think I can add Doc to the list of forgotten memories too.

But if I want to make this work between us, to see what exactly this is, I'm going to have to. Otherwise, it'd be like dumping a bucket of water on the first fire that has kept me warm throughout the night.

CHAPTER TWENTY-THREE

CAMILA

I've never had one of those common fears of heights, spiders, the dark, or any of the other common ones. My fear is one that's easier to come true. One that is hard to prove wrong in being fearful of.

Not that I've ever said it aloud.

I didn't even know this was a fear of mine until Ben. It always nibbled at the back of my mind and made me queasy when we were dating, but it would get stage fright and disappear when Ben pulled me into the shadows. When it was the two of us, the rest of the world didn't seem to matter as much.

It was only in the daylight that my fear resurfaced, making its debut.

Now, standing outside the medical building with the sun beaming down on me, the fear is more prominent than ever.

I inhale a deep breath before releasing it.

You'll be fine, Camila. You aren't here to confess your undying love. You just have to walk in there and---

"Please tell me you aren't here for an emergency," a familiar voice has my eyes popping open to find Ginger, Dr. Robins standing outside the entrance with her hands on her hips.

"No emergency," I promise.

At least, not one she'd consider to be dire. Although, my heart is pounding in my chest and I'm awfully more sweaty than usual.

"I—Is Jason here?"

She eyes me warily for a moment, before nodding hesitantly. "He is."

"Do you think it'd be okay if—"

I don't get to finish my sentence because Sam comes barreling out the door asking Dr. Robins about some kind of procedure. She stops mid-sentence when she spots me.

"Oh, I didn't know you'd be swinging by today, Camila."

"I'm actually here to talk to Jason. If he has a minute, that is."

Instantly, her smile disappears. She's quick to fix it, but the dim in her eyes is still evident. Sam likes him and he's too stubborn to tell her to her face that he's not interested.

Internally, I sigh. Another thing to add to the running list of things I need to discuss.

"He's just finishing up with a patient. I can— Never mind."

She stops when the man in question appears. His head is down as he studies a clipboard in his hand. As if my body is suddenly aware of the magnetic pull, his presence lights a fire inside me.

God, I don't think I will ever get tired or used to how he makes me feel.

Maybe this is all a terrible idea, a mirage from the heat.

"Robins, have you seen…" He trails off when he looks up to find me standing outside of the building with a bright smile on my face.

I give a little, shy wave. Then berate myself internally for it.

What am I? In middle school?

Man, this is embarrassing.

He clears his throat and turns his attention to Dr. Robins. "Have you seen the new vaccine arrive yet?"

My heart drops to the pit of my stomach. All of his focus is on the older woman a few feet from me, but her and Sam are looking at me. Robins with a pitiful sigh I don't quite understand and Sam with a confused gloss to her expression.

Me too, Sam. Me too.

"Not yet," Robins answers him. "I think Johnson just brought it back. I can handle that, though. Why don't you—"

"I got it." He turns on his heel to head back inside, ignoring Dr. Robins' attempt to grab the clipboard from his hand.

Confusion and annoyance dwindling the fire inside me, I take off after him. "Did you forget to put your contacts in today?" I ask him.

He quirks his brow at me as we walk down the hall together. "No."

"What about your ears? Did you clean them this morning?"

Doc stops outside of a closed door, crossing his arms over his chest. "What are you trying to get at, Camila?"

"Nothing. Just worried about your health since you're the only one who didn't see me out there."

"I have work to do." He tries to take off again, but I grab his wrist and stop him.

"What is going on with you?"

"I told you, I—"

"Stop it, Doc." My tone is stern, and I hope it's enough to snap him out of whatever funk he's in. "I have something I want to say and I need to say it now."

He stays silent, watching as a few of the nurses pass by, probably embarrassed at the spectacle I'm creating. Right now, I couldn't care less how we look to the rest of the world.

"Let's talk in private," he mumbles.

Suddenly, it's as if every emotion has come flooding back and a memory of Ben resurfaces in my mind. Being shoved into the shadows just to feel the slightest rush of warmth thrust at me before being left in the dark.

I've been the secret someone keeps locked away. The doll that's only off the shelf when its owner is ready to play with it.

I can't do that again. Not with Doc.

"No," comes out with less confidence than I try to say it with. "I…I—I need to say this here."

He runs a hand through his hair, then rubs at the back of his neck. I hope he's as flustered as he's making me feel. "I can't, Camila."

"What can't you do? Be honest with me? That's all I'm asking of you." My voice is a plea.

His eyes turn sad as he watches the annoyance within me slowly transition into one of exhaustion.

"I didn't come in here to argue with you. I came because…because I like you, Doc. And I didn't want to tell you in a hallway full of people or when we're both obviously so irritated with one another, but I needed to say it before I lost the courage. Even if you don't feel it back."

He lifts his gaze to the ceiling as if he's gathering his patience or trying to rewind time. Trying to make everything I laid out in front of him disappear.

"Doc, I—"

"Why couldn't you have said this weeks ago?" He asks so softly, I almost don't hear it.

"I couldn't stand you weeks ago," I laugh through the words in hopes of lightening the mood.

"That's what would have made it easier to…" Doc let out a long sigh.

I'm frozen to my spot, my nails digging into his skin as I fight for the grounding electricity he usually sends through me, but it's not there. It's not there and my heart is banging against the bars of its cage.

"Camila, I…" His gaze finally meets mine, but I wish it hadn't.

I will my eyes to close, my feet to spin around and sprint out of here, but my body doesn't listen.

"I can't be with you."

My hand falls from his wrist as everything inside me crashes. The organ in my chest slumps against the brick floor of its tower as it watches Doc saunter away with the key in his hand.

"Oh my God," I whisper.

"Camila," he tries to reach for me, but I'm already pulling away.

"I—I can't believe I…"

"I'm sorry." His words are an inaudible echo in my mind. "I'm so sorry, Camila."

This makes me pause. I blink back the water in my eyes. "I'm so embarrassed."

All of these past few weeks…I must have imagined it all and just like with Ben, I let myself think too much into the subtle touches.

Then, as if the locks in my brain are finally clicking, "Oh my God. I've been throwing myself at you for weeks after yelling at you about how you treated Sam."

"No," his hand wraps around my wrist. "Don't do that, Camila. None of this is your fault."

"I made a pass at you," I admit, baffled.

He stays quiet, releasing his grip on me to run his fingers through his hair. I curse the part of myself that wants to do it for him.

Shut up.

"You told me you couldn't be with me in that way. You pulled away every time. Everything you did, *we* did, I…"

I was foolish enough to think too much into it.

"I'm sorry. I'll leave you alone." I stride out of the building, ignoring him calling after me.

My mind is a blind fog as I walk as far away as my feet will carry me.

He should have written in big bold letters on my skin so my heart could read it and understand it. And there's a part of me that's mad he didn't.

The bigger part of me though, isn't angry at him. It's irritated and screaming at *me* because I was stupid enough to ignore all of the flashing neon signs being pointed at me.

God, I'm an idiot.

CHAPTER TWENTY-FOUR

JASON

Three days after I popped the question, a knock came at the front door of Graham and I's apartment. It could have been the pizza Graham ordered or one of the neighbors, but something inside me knew it wasn't.

When I opened the front door to find Jasmine on the other side or with her hair up in a messy bun, her face void of make-up—a rare sight for her---looking as if she barely slept, I knew something was wrong.

"Hey, are—" I couldn't finish my sentence before she barreled passed me and into the apartment.

"Hey, Jaz," Graham came from down the hallway, spotting her. The second he took a look at her appearance, he turned a menacing glare to me. "What did you do?"

I rolled my eyes. "I haven't seen her for three days."

"Clearly you did something, or she wouldn't be here looking…like this." He waved a hand down her frame.

Usually, she'd have a snarky comeback or make a flirty remark. That day, she kept her focus on me and the first thing to come out of her mouth was, "Let's do it."

My heart stopped in my chest. She couldn't possibly mean what I thought she meant. Right? Not after how she stormed out of the restaurant and laughed in my face.

"Can someone please fill me in on what the 'it' she's referring to is?" Graham asked.

Ignoring him, I took a step closer to her. "Are you here to make fun of me? Because I already got the brunt end of it at the restaurant, Jaz, and I've had enough stuff happen at the hospital today that—"

"I'm serious. I thought it over and you made a good case."

"I did?" I asked at the same time Graham said, "What case?"

"There are still some things I think we need to work out and outline. Of course there's the wedding to organize, but we also have to think about after. Where are we living? How many kids? Who will have what shift? I don't want a nanny so don't even think about—"

"Can someone please fill me in on what I missed?" Graham pleaded, interrupting her.

We both turned to him and simultaneously told him to "shut up," although Jasmine was much nicer about it than me. He grumbles a few things but eventually leaves.

When we were alone, she pulled out a chair at the table, sat down, and set her purse on the table. Then, she pulled a notebook out.

"What are you doing?" I sat down across from her.

"If we're going to do this, we need to iron out some details. So," she clicks her pen. "Tell me your wants and absolutely nots and I'll jot them down. Then, I'll set up a meeting with a lawyer so we can—"

"Jaz," I held a hand up, my head getting fuzzy. "Slow down. Why are you here? Because the Jasmine that is sitting in front of me is the not the same one who told me 'No' three days ago."

"I was harsh. I'm sorry."

I leaned back in my chair, crossed my arms, and waited for her to continue.

"You made good points, Jay. I want a family too and, after thinking over what you said, marrying you isn't a horrible idea."

"Even though we aren't in love with each other?"

She tilted her head. "I love you and I trust you. That's all that matters to me."

"What if you're missing out on a chance for that once in a lifetime romance like in those books you read?"

Jasmine is constantly reading romance. She listens to audiobooks in the car or when she's moving. Reads paper books at home and carries a kindle with her everywhere.

"I can't give you that kind of relationship, Jaz."

She nodded, her lips set tight. "I know. If I'd wanted that, I would have trapped Graham years ago."

This made me crack a smile.

Graham is the most romantic guy out there, but he goes about it in all the wrong ways. He overdoes it with thousands of flowers, serenading women, or even buying them pets.

It's amazing he managed to get Piper to fall for him with how shy she is. Honestly, I was surprised she didn't run for the hills sooner.

"I want a family of my own, Jason," Jasmine continues. "I'm tired of coming home to an empty house and having no one to take my jacket when I walk through the door or remind me that it's okay to not look at the calories on the back of a bag or pat my pregnant belly and tell me how much they can't wait to have a little me running around."

I tried to imagine everything she pictured. I imagined me being the one she comes home to or vice versa. I never saw that future with Jasmine before, and I still couldn't see it with us talking about it.

It was like a distant mirage, blurry at the edges, but possible. And that's all I needed to cling on to that possibility.

Attraction comes with time.

I sat up and gestured to her notebook. "Absolutely no cats."

She smiled. "Who do you expect to keep me company while you're at work all day?"

"You run your own company, Jaz. If anyone will need company, it's me."

"You're right." She picked up her pen and started to scribble on the page. "One cat for Jason."

I groaned and wondered if this decision would come back to bite me in the butt.

Now, as I watch Camila run away from me and my heart sinks to the pit of my stomach, I wish I could rewind time.

If I had told her sooner, this might not have happened. We might not even be friends. But the more I learned about her and got closer to her, the more selfish I grew.

Because that's who I am. I'm a selfish asshole who has forced my childhood friend into marrying me and has made the one woman who has ever made me feel comforted and at home by just the touch of her, doubt everything all over again.

The worst part is if I tell her the truth, that I'm engaged, she might think someone picked someone else over her again. That's something I can't do to her.

Even if it means letting her believe I have no feelings for her and the past week or so has been one sided. I can't do to her what her ex did. The thought makes me want to puke.

CHAPTER TWENTY-FIVE

CAMILA

In the city, I'm able to visit Kai's, one of the many friends of my brother, dojo. It's where I learned a handful of moves for my job and it is the place I'd go when lying on the couch inside my dark apartment wasn't enough to battle the demons inside me.

I would visit the dojo so often that Kai wouldn't even bat an eye when I walked in the door. Usually, I went at times when he didn't have classes or was about to close. He simply gave me the key and left.

For the longest time, I'd have trouble performing the moves properly. The scar on my thigh would act up and sting, nearly causing me to fall to the floor on occasion.

But I still got up and punched my fists and kicked my legs. I spun in threatening circles despite having no sparring partner.

Instead, I battled the man who cheated on me. The man who would never let me so much as graze his skin with my nails, let alone spar with me.

I fought the girl who foolishly believed that man would ever be more than a lying and manipulative cheater.

Now, I swing my fists in the air as the dark sky envelopes me. The refuge doesn't have a dojo or even a punching bag. After not being able to turn my mind off and sleep, I threw on a pair of leggings and a sports bra and found the most open space at the refuge, which just so happens to be between the medical and storage buildings.

Luckily, it's two in the morning so the chances of being in anyone's way are slim.

As I kick my feet and ignore the sweat trickling down my face and along my chest, I fight every foolish thing I ever thought about Doc.

I'm so stupid to think he's into me.

I've just been so starved of touch that I lapped up anything he offered me.

"Nice moves."

Instinctively, I turn my fighting stance towards the last man I want to see right now. I'm breathing hard as my chest heaves to suck in lungsful of air.

Doc eyes me with his arms crossed.

Straightening and ignoring the sudden beat in my chest, I ask, "What are you doing here?"

"I was passing by and saw you. Thought I'd stop and say 'hi'."

Something about the way he says it, how casual he is after leaving my heart in its cage, strikes an uncomfortable feeling in my stomach.

"I didn't know you knew how to fight."

"It's part of the job."

He nods, taking in the information. Just when I'm about to brush past him and go back to the tent, anywhere that Doc won't be to see me wallowing because of him, he says the last thing I expect to ever hear from him.

"Teach me."

I scoff in an effort to cover my surprise. My excitement at being able to touch him.

Stop it, Camila.

"What?"

"Teach me a few moves."

"You need help defending yourself?"

He plasters an easy smile on his lips and shrugs. "Humor me."

"I won't go easy on you."

"Don't. I like it rough."

Did he just...?

He turns, yanks his sweatshirt off, and throws it to the ground, not caring where it lands. Without asking for instructions, he gets into position.

I study him, then roll my eyes and come closer. "You're too tense."

This is probably the worst idea I've had since Ben, but something draws me to him. Maybe if I show him a few moves, he will be satisfied and go on his way.

"Don't you need to be tense to throw hard punches?" He asks.

"No. The opposite. Loosen up." I'm within a few feet of him, waiting for him to do it himself.

Like the annoyingly handsome jerk he is, he doesn't move or fix his stance. He's baiting me.

He pretends to be adjusting but does it in all the wrong ways. Giving up, I move closer and place my hand on his back to encourage his spine to bend in the right position.

I'm so lost in the motions, focusing only on how to get it right. Not worried at all about the way his skin sends electric tingles through my fingertips as I do.

Yet, my heart seems to pick up speed. I almost beg it to stop in hopes he won't be able to feel my pulse. Then, I beg that he does. Maybe then he will understand that he isn't the only one who's uncomfortable when we touch. I'm just as frazzled as he is. But for an entirely different reason.

After a moment, my hand pauses on his arm and our eyes catch. I freeze at the longing in his eyes.

No. There is no longing. You can't yearn for someone you barely tolerate.

I blink away the moment and step back, ignoring the chills that now sweeps across me at the loss of contact. I hadn't been cold the entire hour I've been out here, but the second he's out of my reach…

"Good stance," I tell him.

He rolls his shoulders. "What's the first move?"

"I don't know karate or jiu jitsu or any of those."

"I only want to know what you know."

I position myself in a stance across from him and swing my arms into the space between us with specific precision.

He repeats my actions until we are both punching and kicking into the air. Both breathing hard. Both fighting the demons inside us.

Somehow we have gravitated closer to one another. His breaths are falling on my arm, making the hair stand at attention. The tips of my shoes are brushing against his feet. We are within a hairsbreadth of each other. Touching everywhere and nowhere at the same time.

When our cheeks nearly brush together, we stop fighting and try to catch our breath. Except, with him a foot from me, I'm not sure I'll be able to catch mine.

I step away, avoiding his gaze. "Good job."

"Thanks. Am I ready to fight?"

"Who exactly are you fighting?" This was supposed to be a one and done thing. Show him a few moves and send him on his way.

"Mind if I practice with you?"

My muscles tense and my jaw sets. "Why are you here?"

He straightens from his fighting stance and shrugs. "I told you. I came to—"

"Say 'hi'. Got it. Why are you *still* here?"

"Honest?"

"I wouldn't be asking if I wanted a lie." There's no humor in my words, just irritation.

"I think you want to hit me."

My body deflates in surprise as my arms fall from her chest.

"You have some clear agenda against me and I think you want to throw a few punches my way."

Some agenda against him?

Did I or did I not just admit to liking him earlier today? Was he asleep during that conversation?

"You want to fight just so I can hit you?" I ask. "I don't have an agenda against you, Doc. I thought I made that pretty clear this morning."

He rubs at the back of his neck. "I want to fight as an apology."

All of the irritation fizzles out of me like a dying sparker. "You have nothing to apologize for. I'm the one who should be sorry for throwing myself at you."

He gets back into his fighting stance and beckons me towards him with a wave of his curled fist. "Then let's both apologize with our fists."

Chapter Twenty- Six

CAMILA

He's egging me on. He wants me to fight him just so I can bruise him. To make up for this morning. It is such an utterly ridiculous notion, but I couldn't be anymore thrilled to leave a few scars. Whether it is at him or the endless space around us.

"Come on," he repeats as he studies me with a set of his jaw. He's not budging.

Fine.

I move towards him and get into position, mirroring him. Except, his limbs are stiffer than mine and he has his hands raised a little too high.

Usually in Kai's dojo, you'd introduce yourself to your opponent and bow before taking any swings. Doc, however, clearly doesn't want to follow regulations though.

Doing this, indulging Doc is a horrible idea. And yet…

"I'm not going to go easy on you," I tell him.

He smiles, a rare sight that sends a weird flutter in my chest. "I expect nothing less."

I wait for him to swing first. It's best to start as defense—learn your opponent's tells, then move on to offense—but he doesn't make one move. He's waiting for me to do it first.

Fine. If he wants to play that way, then that's how we'll play.

I throw my arm to the right, expecting him to dodge me, but he lets my fist hit his forearm. He doesn't flinch at the contact.

The idea of him throwing this fight, not letting me win in a true and honest way, sends a boiling irritation through my veins.

Who does he think he is?

This time, I throw out a kick. It lands straight into the side of his abdomen, causing him to stumble. He quickly regains his balance and stands up again.

"You sure you want to do this?" I tease.

"Hit me," is all he says.

So I do. I throw a punch, and it lands on the side of his head. I kick his shin and he almost tumbles. This continues—me hitting an unwavering dummy—until I'm breathing harsh, and his form seems to become less human and more of a body bag holding my demons.

The image of a man with ocean eyes the color of blue promises from across the set of a movie production floods my mind.

Punch.

The memory of distracting kisses feather across my collar, my neck, all the way to my jaw.

Kick.

My heart is beating at an erratic rate as the entire scene unfolds before me. It's only when gentle hands wrap around my wrists, stopping me, that I remember who is in front of me.

Jason. Not Ben.

Somehow, it's scarier.

I yank out of his grip and start to swing again. Instead of letting me hit him like before, he grabs my arm this time and slowly lowers my limb back to my side.

Now he wants me to go easy?

I kick my left leg, but he only uses it to draw me closer to him by grabbing my ankle and gently yanking me to him. My breath catches in my throat at his proximity. He's too close.

Using this position to my advantage, I swing my other leg around his waist with my hands wrapped around his neck. I wriggle and pull until he's flat on the floor with me on top.

He groans from the impact, but he doesn't bother pushing me off or fighting back. Instead, he places soft hands on my hips to ensure I don't topple in the process.

"You okay?" He whispers.

I almost laugh. "Shouldn't I be asking *you* that?"

"I'm fine, Bell. No matter what you do to me, I'm fine."

Something about the sincerity in his voice and the way his thumb is tracing circles on my skin through the fabric of my leggings has me frozen.

Why is he letting me do this? Why isn't he fighting back?

Why am *I* letting it happen?

"You shouldn't give me that kind of power." I ignore every emotion coursing through me and release my hold on him to stand.

He tightens his grip on my legs, forcing me back down. The impact causes my head to fall closer towards his face. So closely I can see the flecks of gold in his brown eyes and the pores on his skin.

"You want me to fight back?" His breath fans my lips in the whisper of a kiss.

I'm too frozen to think straight. I need to stand. I need to remove his hands from me and leave. If he wants to fight, then he can stay here. It doesn't have to—

"I'll fight back."

What?

"If you don't want this to be a one-sided battle then I will fight back, but not with fists. Every punch you throw only makes it harder for me to walk away from you, Bellona."

I'm watching the words fall from his mouth as his lips mold the sounds. The urge to reach out and touch his skin, to feel the sentences he's spewing…

"If you want me to fight, then I will. But I'm not going to fight with weapons. That's not what you need."

It's as if a flip switched inside my brain. "What I need?" The question is a whisper on my tongue as I move out of his embrace and stand, too abrupt for him to tighten his hold this time. "What I *need?* What makes you think you know what I need? You don't even know me."

I'm yelling, fuming with smoke practically steaming from my ears. Doc sits up but doesn't stand. He looks exhausted but not from our workout. He looks tired of *me.*

No one asked him to come over here. No one asked him to take each of my hits. In fact, I told him to leave.

"I didn't mean it that way," he finally speaks.

"Please. Save the excuses for someone else and just leave."

"I'm not leaving."

God, he's such an asshole. "Do you not know when you aren't wanted? I can't take all of this back and forth, Jason. Was my embarrassment this morning not enough for you?"

He freezes, not one ounce of him making even the tiniest movement. I know my words were harsh, but I wasn't mean.

I glance around us as if something in the void around us will give me an answer as to why he isn't saying anything.

"What?" I force out.

He stands and takes one step towards me, then stops a foot away when he sees me eyeing his movements. "You...you called me *Jason*."

I hadn't even noticed, but I roll my eyes at his childness despite the weird flip in my stomach. Seriously? "It's your name, isn't it?"

"Yes, but you've never called me it." As if losing all sense of self control, he strides towards me.

I back up, but each step he takes is worth two of mine. He's too fast. Too fast and I have no—

My feet snag in a hole on the ground, nearly causing me to stumble, but it stops my steps instead and forces me to crane my head upwards to meet his stare properly.

"Say it again," he whispers as he sets his hand on my exposed waist with the gentlest touch.

"What?" It's the only word I can muster. The only one that makes any sense right now.

He's staring at my lips, and I wonder if he's going to kiss me. My heart is beating too fast to think. Too fast to even consider the possibility. But he is. He's studying my mouth as though it is an intricate puzzle.

It's so different from Ben. By now, Ben would have ripped my clothes to shreds long before I had the chance to so much as utter a word.

Doc, I'm learning, likes to take his time.

Not that this is meant to lead anywhere.

"My name," he whispers. So soft I almost don't hear it. "Say my name." His eyes flick up to mine. "Please."

I'm frozen with every other thought out of my mind. He's not touching me. In fact, he's still a foot from me. He doesn't have me completely cornered and there's still room for me to escape.

I wonder if he did that intentionally. Giving me an out. Then, I remember who's standing in front of me and I know: he did.

My mouth opens to say his name and grant him with the one thing he seems to be starved of. The word is on my tongue and his eyes flick back to my parting lips when a memory comes back to me.

I can't be with you.

Instead of saying what he wants, I say, "You don't like me, Doc, so please stop acting like you do."

He leans his forehead against mine and closes his eyes, taking in a small breath. It's taking everything in me to not lean my head up the slightest inch it needs for my lips to land on his.

"I'm sorry." All too soon he pulls away and walks to his discarded jacket.

Cold air consumes my skin as I try to regain my breathing. I blink the space back into sight in an attempt to right my senses.

With his back still facing me and his jacket clenched tightly in one fist as his side, he looks at me over his shoulder. I pray to God I don't look as completely wrecked as I feel.

"I didn't mean to confuse you," he whispers, but it rings in my ears. "You...you drive me crazy and it's the first time I've ever felt out of control. I'm sorry," is the last thing he says before he saunters away and leaves me in the dark.

CHAPTER TWENTY-SEVEN

JASON

"Last one," Johnson claims as he throws the last suitcase into the back of the car.

We all go home today. Four months ago, I looked forward to this day. I couldn't wait to get back and start a family with Jasmine.

Now, I almost wish there was an emergency to keep us here. My fingers are still crossed in hopes of a weather emergency.

I never technically cheated on Jasmine, not physically, but my heart was never fully attached to hers.

I'm about to hop inside the car when I hear his voice shouting at me.

"Who the hell do you think you are?" Paxton grabs the collar of my shirt. "You think you can just make passes at my sister and then go about your day like nothing happened?"

He raises his fist, but I don't say or do anything to stop him. I deserve everything he has to throw at me. Not only have I been a confusing asshole to Camila, but I also practically cheated on Jasmine.

I convinced her to marry me and start a life with me. She's moving us into a house as we speak and is going to be at the airport to pick me up in less than twenty-four hours.

She's been nothing but dutiful and kind and perfect, while I've been falling for someone else behind her back.

And I didn't even have the courage to tell her over the phone the other day.

The guilt eats me alive as Paxton's stews in front of me. His face is covered in sweat, but it's hard to tell if it's from the heat or his anger or both.

"Paxton," a familiar voice calls from behind him.

It makes my heart sink, but only because of how void of all emotion it sounds. *I did that.*

I meet Paxton's stare, willing him to go through with it. Maybe if he knocks me out hard enough, all of this will become one crazy dream.

But he lowers his fist and lets go. "I should beat you to a pulp," he mumbles to me so only I can hear.

Then, he steps away, and his sister appears behind him. She steps closer to me, studying my face and chest for any bruises. "Are you okay?"

After I played hot and cold with her, turned her down, embarrassed her, backed her into a corner, and almost kissed her because she said *my name,* she's still caring for me.

I duck my head, too guilt ridden to meet her eyes, and climb into the vehicle. Without so much as a word to either of them, I speed off towards the airport and pray to God my seat is miles from hers.

Apparently, God has a dark sense of humor because my seat is the middle seat beside Camila's window seat.

Fan-fucking-tastic.

She must notice me standing at the edge of the aisle because her head turns from the window to find me. She offers me a small smile, which is meant to comfort me, I guess, but it only makes me want to puke.

How can someone be so sweet to someone so vile?

I decide to ask someone to switch seats with me when I spin around to find a flight attendant in my way. "Please take your seat, Sir. We will be taking off soon."

Internally cursing this plane and myself, I stuff my bag up top and plop down in the seat beside Camila.

So far, the person who's supposed to sit beside me isn't here yet. Maybe I can convince them to trade places with me.

I could say I get motion sickness or have the bladder of a woman in her third trimester and need easy access to the bathroom.

Or I could shoot a quick text to Robins and offer to take all of the "stinky patients" as she calls them for a month if she trades spots with me.

I'm about to pull my phone out and do just that when Camila says, "You don't have to avoid me."

My gaze meets hers. Did I say my thoughts aloud?

"I'm not going to jump you simply because you're a foot from me. Believe it or not, I have self-control, Doc."

Here I am trying to find a way out of sitting next to her, so I don't make her any more uncomfortable than she already is and yet, doing so is doing the exact opposite.

"I'm not worried you're going to jump me, Bell."

She winces. "Can you stop calling me that please?"

"Why?" It's not an insult. Is she taking it as one?

"Because it makes me think you care for me in the way I care for you."

My mouth twists into a frown as I turn my attention away. It's on the tip of my tongue to tell her that she's wrong. That I do care for her, probably more than she cares for me, but it's stuck.

It's tethered to my heart who is yanking back inside.

I can't tell her until I talk to Jasmine. Hell, I probably can't ever tell Camila how I really feel about her because I made a promise to Jasmine.

And, while I haven't been the best fiancé these past few months, I'm not going to break up with Jasmine for my own selfish reasons.

I've been selfish enough as it is already.

So I pull out a pair of headphones and drown out the rest of the rest of the world the only way I know how.

CHAPTER TWENTY-EIGHT

JASON

Something hits my leg with a crinkling sound, startling me awake. I open my eyes to find a kid peering over the seat in front of me with a goofy grin on his face. His orange, curly hair is splayed out like he slept funny.

I straighten and pick the bag of goldfish off the floor before passing them to him. "I think you dropped this, buddy" I say softly.

He giggles like it's the funniest thing he's heard.

Then, a woman's face appears beside him as she gives me the most apologetic look. "I'm so sorry. He slept the whole way to the airport in the car and is wired too much to actually sleep."

I give her a soft smile. "It's okay."

"I hope he didn't wake you."

"He didn't. I can't sleep on planes either." It's a lie, but it makes the embarrassed apology leave her expression.

She must grab her son because he disappears and so does she. I settle back in my seat stretching my legs. In the process, my gaze flicks to the only other person in the row—apparently the person who reserved the seat beside me didn't show; Or the universe is really against me.

Her hair is stuck to the side of her face with sweat as she leans her head against the window. There's a wrinkle between her brows, but it's hard to tell if it's because of her discomfort or if she's having a bad dream.

The air kicks on above us and she adjusts her position to shift closer to the window and further from the cool air.

Her feet are tucked underneath her, her worn out shoes long forgotten on the floor by my feet.

She's curled herself into a ball and my chest aches at the thought that she's lying this way because of me. Because she's trying to escape me.

Camila is so breathtakingly beautiful, and I can't even tell her that.

My fingers itch to reach out and tuck the falling strands of her hair behind her ear or feel how soft those lips I'll never be able to touch are. Although, they look a little chapped from my position.

Her head leans forward, putting her neck at an awkward angle and it becomes too much to bear any longer.

Swallowing my hesitation, I reach up to tug my hoodie off. Then I fold and roll it to make the best makeshift pillow I can. I'll remove it before she wakes up so I'm not sending her any more mixed signals.

When I'm satisfied, I unbuckle my seatbelt and lean over her to gently lift her head and prop the hoodie beneath her.

Next, I adjust the vents above us, so they aren't blowing in her direction anymore. Then, as quietly as is humanly possible, I lift the armrests up between us so there's no longer a barrier. As I slide into the aisle seat, I slowly pull her legs with me so she has more wiggle room to be comfortable.

There's still at least another twelve hours to this flight and there is no way I'm letting her sleep in a ball for that long.

When she's better situated and I'm in my new seat, I let my eyes rake over her one more time. There's a hint of drool spilling from her mouth and onto my hoodie.

A laugh bubbles out of me, but I don't realize it until I hear it.

She's so strange, yet ridiculously adorable that it makes my heart swell. Camila is so breathtakingly beautiful I don't know how I'm going to face the woman waiting for me in the city.

When we finally land and leave the plane, Camila stops me with her hand outstretched between us. I quirk a brow at her, staring at the same hand I dreamed of taking the entire flight.

"I'm proposing a second truce."

"When did we go to war again?"

She chuckles and it echoes in my bones. "Probably around the time I embarrassed myself in front of you. Look, we don't have to be best friends or even see each other again if you don't want to. I'm just suggesting that we put it all behind us."

I shift on my feet. As much as I wish I had better self-control, there's not an ounce of me that wants to forget our time together. I want to latch onto it and tie it up so it can never leave. I want more memories. I want more of *her.*

But I can't have that because I made a promise and I may be selfish, but I'm not a bad businessman.

Swallowing the lump in my throat, I place my hand in hers, trying to ignore the electric shock of her touch and how perfectly her hand fits in mine, as we shake on the second truce we've made in a month.

She drops my hand far too quickly and points a thumb over her shoulder. "I should probably get going. My friend's waiting for me. But don't be a stranger, Doc."

Doc. Not Jason or even nothing at all, but Doc.

I've never hated a word more than I hate that one. People have given me all kinds of names over the years, especially since I'm a doctor who deals with patients in extreme pain, but none of those names have stung as much as this one does.

I open my mouth to ask—demand she never call me that again when someone bumps into my back and causes me to stumble towards her.

One of her hands lands on my chest while the other clutches my arm, keeping me stable. Being near her is the only thing that has ever made me feel unstable. She grounds me, but at the same time runs me wild with enough energy to do laps around the airport.

"You okay?" She gives me a small, genuine smile that makes my chest constrict.

No. I'm not okay at all.

"Yeah." I step back from her touch as her arms fall back at her sides.

"Well, I'll see you later then. Or I won't. Truce?"

I nod and say the only thing my tongue is strong enough to push out, "Truce."

Then, without so much as a warning or anything else uttered between us, Camila takes off in the other direction, dragging my heart along with her.

CHAPTER TWENTY-NINE

CAMILA

"Hey, hot stuff," Lily greets me outside of the airport as she leans against an SUV.

"Hi," I'm all smiles and well rested and *happy* as I take the coffee she offers me. When I take a sip, I sigh in contempt. "You know me so well."

She eyes me warily with an arched brow and her finger twisting in her long blonde hair. "Who are you and what have you done with my best friend?"

I laugh. "Oh, don't be dramatic."

"You seem in a much better mood than you left in. Maybe Paxton's idea wasn't half bad."

"Did you just compliment my brother?" I follow her to the trunk with my suitcase.

"You have to appreciate your enemy's moves if you're ever going to earn enough of their trust to stab the knife in their back."

"Brutal."

She shrugs. "I've been on a thriller kick."

She opens the trunk of the car for me to throw my suitcase inside before we both climb in. I barely have enough time to buckle my seat and set the coffee in the cup holder before the interrogation starts.

"Tell me everything."

I slide my shoes off my feet and pull my legs up underneath me. "There's not much to tell."

Lily pulls out of her spot and onto the road, cutting off a car in the process. She ignores their honking. "Aren't you the woman who called me a week ago with heart eyes?"

"You couldn't see me. How do you know if I had heart eyes or not?"

"I didn't until just now."

"Shut up."

She laughs and starts to adjust the radio. "So? Tell me more about this *doctor.*" The title comes off her tongue flirtatiously.

"Well, I did what you said, but…it kind of backfired."

"Oh, Hun." She reaches a hand to grip my thigh in a reassuring touch, the bracelets on her wrist clanging together from the movement. "Should we find his car and slash his tires? Or steal the battery? I know some—"

"Lily."

She lets one hand off the wheel long enough to raise her hand and point a finger at the roof. "You're right. That would look too suspicious. We should hire an assassin."

I'm laughing so hard it shocks her enough to give me a curious glance from the corner of her eye. "How about we stick with something more normal?" I ask when I've sobered up.

"Fine, but just know that if my stories lack creativity, it's your fault."

"Duly noted. So, tell me about you. What's been going on this past month?"

"Same old. Same old."

I shift in my seat to face her so my back is half against the seat and half against the door. "You get mad at *me* for not delving into detail."

She starts to adjust the air conditioning for the second time, changing it so it blows on our upper body and not our feet. "You really want to know?"

"Why wouldn't I? Aren't friends supposed to ask about each other?"

Lily stays quiet for a moment and something uneasy settles into my chest. I rub at the spot in hopes of relieving the tension.

When she finally speaks, I'm not ready for what she has to say. "Friends do, but we aren't normal friends, Cam. Never have been."

Instantly, I wish I could scoop her up into a giant hug and erase the sad tone in her words. Lily and I have never hugged, but the urge to show her how much she means to me makes my fingers itch.

We aren't normal friends. We talk about problems and complain with one another, but we never actually address what's under the surface or what is really bothering us. If I'm being honest, I rarely ever ask her about her life in hopes of an honest answer. I only ever do it out of obligation.

Now, as I sit in the passenger seat of her dad's car, I realize how much of a terrible friend I have been over the past few years. Even when Ben and I were dating, I treated Lily more like an annoying cousin that you only see out of obligation than an actual friend.

Which is all clearer to me because of how someone—who is not a friend or someone who owes me anything—treated me the past months.

Shaking all of the memories with Doc away, I focus on Lily.

"I'm sorry. I haven't been a great friend for—well, I don't even know how long, but it's not an excuse."

We come to a stoplight and Lily pins me with a stare. "What happened to you on this trip?"

I bite back the smile tugging on my lips. It's not a what but a who. Doc happened. He showed me a different side of life. While I'm still learning how to get passed Ben and move on, I've never felt more rejuvenated and clearer headed than I do now

There's a lot I need to do differently, starting with Lily. She's the one and only friend who has stuck by me all these years.

She doesn't so much as bat an eye at how snarky and defensive I can be. Instead, she just continues to make playful jabs until my guard falls, and the laughter takes its place.

Paxton's not her biggest fan, but he doesn't know her like I do. He has no clue how wonderful of a person she truly is.

Yeah, she can be eccentric and overwhelming sometimes, but that's just who Lily is. It's one of the things I adore the most about her.

"I'm reviving the real me," I answer her early question.

"Wow," she whistles. "And you came back philosophical? Maybe I should go on a trip."

I laugh. "I'll call Paxton and set it up."

"You do that and I will throw away the croissants I brought you."

"You brought me croissants?"

She grins and tilts her head to the back. I unbuckle my seatbelt and reach into the back for the white paper bag labeled "Oliver's".

"Is this from that new Italian restaurant?"

"Mhmm."

I dig my hand inside, pulling out the warm treat. It's chocolate: my favorite. Without hesitating, I tear a piece off and stuff it into my mouth.

"Oh my God," I moan around the food in my mouth. "This is like baked heaven."

"I know, right? Wanna know the best part?"

I nod as I devour more of the croissant.

"You're staring at the new best friend of said croissant maker-cooker-thing."

Another thing about Lily: she may be a writer, but she's not very good with words verbally. I once witnessed her try to direct a delivery man to her parent's house by differentiating the roads between "windy" and "short".

Safe to say he got lost at least three times and never delivered to her again.

"Best friend, huh?" I ask.

"Well, maybe not best friend. Hazel and Piper are actually pretty tight in their friendship. I don't think they've ever even fought over a boy."

"Healthy."

She gives me a look of disbelief. "That's what I said!"

Someone honks their horn at us as Lily comes to an abrupt stop at another set of traffic lights. Her arm comes out to block the front of me as we lean forward, but neither of us bats an eye or stops the conversation.

"Anyway, I went there to eat the other day and met the brilliant Pastry Chef, Hazel. We got to talking and it turns out we have a lot in common. She invited me out for drinks with her friends Piper and Graham, and now I have an in for both free desserts and free drinks."

"How do the drinks fit into this equation?" I adjust the vents blowing cold air on me so they aim towards the window instead.

"Graham works as a bartender. He's Piper's boyfriend. Hints: free drinks."

"His boss doesn't care?"

"Oh, Sebastian—he's Italian by the way—" she winks at this part. "He hates it. Nearly fired Graham three times these past two weeks."

"And he didn't because?"

She shrugs. "No clue. My guess though? He's secretly in love with Graham."

This makes me choke on the bite of croissant in my mouth. "You're insane."

"Why? A guy can't be in love with another guy?"

"I didn't say that, but something tells me the only reason you suspect that is because it's the inspiration for one of your books."

"Guilty as charged."

We trail off in our conversation. Talking about everything and nothing as she drives me home. She mentions going out with Piper and Hazel sometime soon, and I agree without a flicker of hesitation.

Tomorrow, I will have to get back to reality. I'll have to meet Kyra and start looking for a job on the side in between gigs. I'll have to figure out a way to keep the lights on in my apartment.

For now, though, I enjoy my time with the friend I've been too self-absorbed to even ask "how are you" to.

The one thing I don't think about: Doc. Or, at least, I try not to, but he's still lurking in the back of my mind.

He doesn't want anything to do with me. That much was clear when I woke up on the plane to find him in the furthest seat from me. When we landed, he couldn't escape any faster.

Yet, something drew me to stop him from walking away completely so I could call a second truce. Some part of me hoped he changed his mind and would ask for my number or any of my socials. But none of that happened.

Instead, he shook my hand and went about his day like I was just another task on his list.

It shouldn't, but it still hurts.

CHAPTER THIRTY

JASON

> **Truce**: an agreement between enemies or opponents to stop fighting for a certain time.
> **Enemies**: a person who is actively opposed or hostile to someone.
> **Hostile**: marked by malevolence.
> **Hostile**: openly opposed or resisting.

These words filter through my mind as I watch the scenery of the crowded streets slowly pass by from the passenger seat of Jasmine's car. Despite her father's insistence, she prefers to drive herself around instead of her assistant.

She picked me up from the airport about fifteen minutes ago and I know I should say something, anything, but I can't bring myself to utter more than one word.

"How did the trip go?" *Good.*

"How was the flight?" *Fine.*

"Should we stop for sushi on the way?" *Sure.*

The instinct to give Jasmine more, be a better companion in this car ride, is burning inside, but it's not as gripping as the last interaction I had with Camila.

Truce. She called a second truce as if the first one had disappeared.

A truce is between two enemies, though, and enemies are hostile. Camila is far from a foe and is the gentlest person I've met.

The last thing I want to call Camila is my enemy.

But I can't refer to her as anything more than a friend. Hell, even that feels wrong. A friend is someone you can call up at any moment or can hang out with or is there for you. I don't have any way of contacting Camila unless I call Paxton and ask for her number. Considering how he felt about me before I got on the plane, that's not really a viable option.

Stop it, Jason, I reprimand myself. *You have no business even considering contacting her when you are—*

Engaged.

Engaged to Jasmine. The woman I haven't so much as said 'hi' to since I got off the plane. The woman who mapped her busy schedule out so she had time to pick me up from the airport and take me home.

I'm a jerk.

I shift in my seat and turn my head towards her. "Thanks for picking me up."

She doesn't glance in my direction, too focused on the road, but I see the crease appear on her forehead. "Did Jason Michael Young just say, 'thank you'?"

I roll my eyes and stretch my legs as I sink a little further into the seat.

Jasmine laughs at her own joke before reaching over to tap my thigh with her hand. It doesn't escape my notice that there's no electricity shooting from her fingertips and into my bloodstream.

I shift uncomfortably under her touch, but she doesn't seem to notice as she takes her hand back.

"I'm just kidding. You are very much welcome, Fiancé."

Fighting the wince, I say, "How's the house?"

"The appraiser came by last week and approved everything. It's in tip top shape—his words, not mine—so Graham, Piper, and Hazel have been helping me move everything."

Part of our agreement was to buy a house, not a condo, with a big yard and enough bedrooms for at least two or three kids, as well as enough space for Jasmine and I to have time alone. By time alone, I mean us individually and not intimately together.

She will have an office suiting her needs and I will have an office matching mine. We decided to sleep in the same bed after the wedding, especially since we will need to be…doing things. That's how one creates a family, I guess.

This part of our agreement, though, is the one I'm looking forward to the least. Being intimate with Jasmine—hell, just hugging her or holding her hand, makes me nauseas.

But this will all pass. It has to pass.

This is ultimately a business deal to provide each other the stability we need. Nothing more.

Since Mother and Jasmine are planning for the wedding to happen in August—about two weeks from now—Jasmine took the brunt of the moving while I was away.

"How much is left?" I ask.

"I've gotten everything out of my apartment, except for my daily essentials since I will still be living out of it for the next few weeks. We moved the big stuff out of your place too, but I left the personal items and clothes for you. Figured you'd want to move that on your own."

I nod, picturing how barren the apartment will be when I get there. The last day of living in the apartment is approaching must faster than I anticipated.

This weekend is when we will be announcing our engagement. Mother and Jasmine have everything all planned out and all I have to do is show up in a suit and wear my best smile.

We would have announced our engagement sooner, but going across the globe for three months isn't ideal for a bride who claims it will not be a great look for her to be announcing her engagement without the groom present.

As I sit in this too tightly built car, I wish the party would have already happened.

"Are you nervous at all?"

We stop at a red light, and she glances at me, her long hair ponytail in the process. "Isn't the bride supposed to get cold feet, not the groom?"

I don't say anything because I'm not sure what to say. What does one say when they are having doubts about marrying the woman they proposed to? The same woman who laid out every one reason this would be a bad idea and gave me at least a dozen chances to exit this deal but shook my hand anyway when I signed on the dotted line.

"What's going on, Jay? You've been off since the moment I picked you up."

"Nothing," I lie. Then, because this is my problem to deal with and be a man about, I lie again. "Just worried Graham is going to show up in the most ridiculous tux."

She laughs. "Oh, he hundred percent is. If you had more friends, I'd say you could try swapping your best man."

I lean my head back against the headrest and close my eyes. "Do you think Sebastian will do it?"

Sebastian is Graham's boss and the owner of *Last Call*, a bar we all frequent.

"I bet he'd love to have one up on Graham with how often Graham steals from him."

Another thing about my best friend: he likes to "borrow" things in the effort of helping others. Hazel, Piper's friend, is a baker. For the longest time, Graham would pay her in ingredients he took from the bar in exchange for her desserts.

There's no doubt in my mind that Sebastian knows what Graham's been up to, but he hasn't so much as threatened to fire Graham.

Jasmine scoffs. "I don't think Sebastian would be able to handle being at the front of the room without turning a bright red. He can't even talk to me for more than five seconds without fumbling over his words, let alone stand across from me at the altar."

This makes me open my eyes and quirk a brow at her.

Jasmine has met Sebastian before, but as far as I know, they've always been friends of each other's friends and nothing even remotely closer. And Sebastian is far from being nervous around women.

He could give Graham a run for his money with how easily he flirts with a crowd without so much as a flicker of doubt.

I don't voice any of this, though, because there's one part of her statement that catches more of my attention.

"Wouldn't I be the one standing opposite you at the altar?"

Her grip adjusts on the steering wheel, one of her tells, before she produces a fake laugh. "Of course, but he'd be right behind you."

It's on the tip of my tongue to ask if something happened while I was away, but I don't voice it aloud. Not when I'm the one who's guilty of falling for the person I won't be spending the rest of my life with.

CHAPTER THIRTY-ONE

CAMILA

I wake up to the sound of my alarm rather than the light creeping through the window. Stretching, I reach over to turn it off and squeeze my eyes tighter.

Get up, I tell myself.

It's Wednesday, a few days after getting back, and the beginning of a fresh start. Step one: get off the couch and open the curtains.

Reminding myself of the future I want seems to do the trick enough to force myself up on my knees and reach over the back of the couch to rip open the curtains, sunlight flooding into the room.

My eyes squint at the brightness, but I don't shy away from it. Instead, I open the window and breathe in the fresh air, forcing a smile on my face.

I'm not content or happy in the slightest, but I will be. And I have always believed in faking it 'til you make it.

I will be better. It just takes time.

I stand from the couch and pad towards the fridge, pulling out an orange not covered in mold.

As my nails tear into it, my gaze lands on the disheveled mess of my apartment. There are stacks of scripts and mail in the corner, a handful of untouched books on a broken shelf, at least ten takeout containers littered everywhere, and a few piles of clothing ranging from clean to dirty. At this point, I'm not sure which pile is which.

Out of all of that, my gaze snags on a black box in the corner.

It's a box of all of Ben's things. He was the last guy I ever let into this apartment, minus Paxton. Folding the ends of the box down, I am met with our memories, the ones I tried so desperately to rid myself of.

Movie tickets from the movie we snuck into dressed in disguise. A stack of sticky notes he left around the apartment for me. An outfit he would change into every time he was here.

I held on to this stuff in the hope that he would one day show up at my door and I could either shove it in his face or he would have more to add to it. I hoped he would actually tell me it would just be me and him now and there is no more Elizabeth.

The memory burns into me but I'm too numb to care. Instead, before giving myself a chance to second guess, I find things around the apartment and shove them inside too.

Books he gifted me. Jewelry he bought. Candles I purchased for our nights in—although every night with him was inside. A stupid magnet from his trip to Barcelona. I throw all of it and more into the box.

Then, I find trash bags and do the same with other stuff. Clothes I don't wear, old food, shoes that don't fit, and knickknacks I only kept to be nice to the gifter. Everything gets thrown into bags.

In the process, my phone rings with Lily's name. "Hey," I answer before she has a chance to say anything, "you got any plans today?"

"Just to be at your service today for whatever you need."

"Great." I stand straighter and stare at the outdated pullout couch and broken shelf beside it. "I'm going to need some muscles."

The next step in my plan to a better me is finding a job. After I talk to Kyra, that is.

I push open the door to her office, not bothering to knock since it's already cracked open a hair and Kyra isn't the type who sits at her desk, waiting for her secretary to buzz her about an appointment. Partially because her office is an extra storage room on the second floor of a building rented out to various businesses. This floor is for CraftyCindies, a group of older women who make bracelets out of flowers. I'm pretty sure all of their names are Cindy too.

When the door is open, Kyra comes into view as she bounces on an exercise trampoline behind her desk. The room is the size of a shoe box and Kyra makes use of every inch.

"Camila," she greets in between breaths. "You're back."

"Got back yesterday." I grab the foldable chair where it's leaning against the wall and unfold it to sit across from her on the other side of her desk, nearly pinching my finger in the process.

"Give…me just…twenty…seconds," she breathes out.

Her brown hair is matted around her face and drops of sweat trickle down the column of her neck. She must have been at it for a while with how evident it is.

After about five more bounces, she steps off the trampoline, nearly losing her balance in the process, and wipes at the sweat with a towel she left on her desk.

"Alright," she throws the towel around her shoulders. "How can I help ya', darlin'?"

"I was wondering if any more jobs came through. I know the last time we spoke, you weren't having any luck, but…I thought it wouldn't hurt to ask."

Kyra takes a seat at her end of the desk, and when she starts to bounce again, I immediately assume she's sitting on a yoga ball. She opens her laptop and types something. Then taps her fingernails against the desk. Then types again.

I wait patiently in my spot, used to her disorganization at this point. In the past, I'd be fuming with annoyance and impatience, but now, everything just feels *lighter*.

Could be because of the pile of junk I divvied up between donations and the dumpster.

"A'right!" She does one final tap before twisting the computer to face me. "I actually had something come through the other day and the director would love to meet with you to discuss."

A light of hope flickers inside me. "What's the role?"

"You'd be the double for one of the side characters in an upcomin' action movie. I think there's…yes! You'll be battling a combination between dinosaurs and sharks. It's for the side role of 'Sarah.'"

Normally, I'd shake my head and leave. It's been my dream to be a stunt double and a pretty successful one at that. I didn't want to waste my time doing anything else, especially in a movie with some dinosaur-shark mix.

After being away for a month, watching Paxton and Doc and everyone else help so many people…

I sit up straighter, rolling my shoulders, and lie through my teeth, "Sounds perfect. When can I meet with them?"

"This weekend actually. At the Violet Hotel. I'll set it up and send you the details."

CHAPTER THIRTY- TWO

CAMILA

A red sedan flips in the air, rolling as it travels and lands within a foot from me. Luckily, I sprint at the perfect speed to be out of the danger zone by a hairline. My breaths come out ragged and forced as I stare at the sight behind me, sucking in a lungful of the humid air.

Despite all of the equipment around, not one fan or air conditioner is blowing in this direction.

I wait and imagine the buildings around me are blocked by a blurry haze from the sedan catching on fire. The flames almost feel real with how hot my skin is.

"Cut!"

The room comes into focus as my imagination fades away. In place of the burning city is one of the large conference rooms of the Violet Hotel, except almost all of the tables are missing.

One long table is at the entrance of the room, blocking the door, with the director and a few other crew members seated at it and facing me.

Somehow they managed to get a green screen and a few pieces of equipment here for me to audition with. I've done auditions in a hotel before, but never has it consisted of real scaling and a production set up.

The producer of this movie must have even more pull and seniority than I thought possible.

Standing from my crouched position, my muscles start to ache at the effort. Stretching did not fit into today's schedule.

The team in front of me wears smiles on their faces as the director snaps his hands instead of clapping.

I try to catch my breath and not appear out of shape.

"Wonderful," the director compliments. "Thank you for coming, Camila. I will have my assistant coordinate with your agent."

There is no clear answer in his statement to whether or not I have the part and will be receiving paychecks for the next few months, but I've learned questioning and demanding information only makes the directors put you on a 'no hire' list.

So I nod, thank them for their time, and exit the room.

This isn't the type of movie I usually do for stunts, but it's the only one that has offered me an audition in the past few months, which is all I can ask for.

I'm not broke, but my savings only have so much in it before I will have to make a decision on if I cherish water more than electric or vice versa.

If this doesn't pan out and they decide to go with someone else, I'll have to apply for a part time job at one of the businesses around my apartment. I have more experience being a waitress than I do in my actual profession.

As the door to the conference room clicks close behind me and I turn around in the hallway, I only take about three steps before I stop dead in my tracks.

I must be delusional or sick or maybe I didn't drink enough water today because the sight before me must be a mirage.

There's no other explanation for the man in a suit with a beautiful woman in a pale blue gown and a long braid of hair over her shoulder, hanging on his arm. Although, she appears much more comfortable than him so maybe it's the other way around and she's the one leading him.

Either way, my eyes nearly bug out at the sight.

My father used to tell me how much the universe loves to trick people and create chaos. He used to tell me about how the stars were once kids who wished to be famous. So the universe made them a deal: fame for their youth and fun.

Then the universe swept the kids into the sky, so they are forever remembered and looked at while the universe uses their youthful antics to cause more ruckus.

Now, as I stare frozen at the man I thought I'd never see again, I can't help but feel like this is all one big childish prank.

My theory is proved even further when Doc's gaze swings toward this end of the hall and his attention settles on me.

Even from this distance, I can *feel* his body stiffen, even from this distance. There's this strong urge inside me to yell across the hall at him, "I'm not going to embarrass you in front of your date," but I don't.

Instead, I remind my heart of how foolish it's been in the past, duck my head, and stride as fast as I possibly can out of here.

Each step echoes in my mind like a stomping reminder of the last time I ran away from a man.

Almost two years ago, I knocked on the door to Ben's condo apartment. He gave me the key code to get in, but he only wanted me to use it in case of emergency. So far, there had never been an emergency.

No one answered so I rang the bell again, adjusting the black straps to my top as I waited. Normally, I wouldn't have worn such a revealing outfit out, but since my only destination was Ben's, it didn't matter.

I had no doubt he would peel off whatever I wore anyway. Except, that day I hoped it would be after we talked.

The show ended a few months prior and, a week after that, so did the publicizing for it. Meaning, Ben could finally end things with Elizabeth. It's a day I waited for since the moment he first kissed me after we went out for drinks at the start of our show.

One and a half years later, there we were.

My finger pushed on the doorbell once more, waiting. I checked inside my purse, ensuring the envelope with tickets is still inside. In celebration of this big day, I decided to surprise Ben with a trip. I didn't have money like he did, but money seemed little in comparison to the plans I had.

This was our first chance to be seen in public or do *anything* in public besides our occasional glances at one another.

The energy coursed through me like a jolt. When there was still no response, I typed in the code and carefully opened the door.

It was only ten in the morning, and he had no meetings or shoots scheduled for the day. His first day off in a while so it wouldn't be surprising if he was still sleeping.

Quietly, I slipped out of my converse and crept towards his bedroom. He was usually the one to sneak up on me, but not then. That day I—

Muffled noises crept through his bedroom door. Ben groaned and instantly I wondered if he had injured himself. I made a motion to quicken my pace, but then I heard a moan. A *woman's* moan.

I froze, my heart sinking into the pit of my stomach as I tried to tell myself that I must have heard things. It had to be an illusion. Maybe he had the TV playing and it happened to be a particularly inappropriate scene.

Biting my lip, I slowly pushed the door open a crack wider, hoping to find him in bed with a remote in his hand.

My blood turned cold at the sight through the crevice. Ben, the man I thought would be my forever, was on top of a woman. To make matters worse, he screamed the name "Elizabeth."

No.

I shook my head, biting back the lump in my throat.

He said they weren't real. It was all publicity. He said—

My foot bumped into an end table as I backed up, causing a jagged ceramic vase to fall. Quickly I caught it to prevent it from crashing and making noise.

He can't know I am here. *She* can't know.

I set it back carefully, then booked it to the door, grabbing my shoes, and running into the hall.

It's only when I was in the stairwell, deciding the elevator is too cramped, that I realized my breaths became shallow. Instantly, it was like every bottled emotion burst and decided to swarm within me.

Every memory of Ben and I came flooding back like a tsunami. Our first kiss in a secluded hallway with beer on his breath. His fingers blazing a trail of promises across my skin in the dark. His bubbly laugh when I'd say something ridiculous or mine when he'd tickle my ribs.

I covered my mouth with my hand, hoping to conceal the sobs wracking my body. As I sank to the ground, I felt it.

My vision blurred from the tears, but I noticed a gash on my thigh. The vase must have cut me as it fell, but I was too focused on hiding to realize.

Even when he deceived me, I hid.

God, I was such a coward.

My sobs echoed in the stairwell, mocking me.

I'm such a stupid, worthless, coward, I repeated in my mind over and over.

Why did I ever think he was telling the truth?

Then I realized, as my head stayed buried on top of my bent knees, the blood from the cut bleeding into my clothing, just how fucking stupid I am.

The worst part: I still hoped he would burst through the door to the stairwell—somehow knowing I was in his apartment—wrap me up in his arms and tell me everything would be okay. That what I saw was all part of a plan. That I imagined everything and this was all some crazy nightmare.

That I was still the one he wanted.

But the door to the stairwell never opened and the only soothing sounds around me were the horrid sobs escaping me.

As my stomach sours, the memory switches to a different, more recent one. One where I lift my head to find myself not cowering in the corner of a stairwell, but wrapped in arms holding me so tight that every broken part of me is able to stitch back together.

Memories sift in and out of my mind of fingers intertwining with my mine and squeezing, sitting on a cold bench and staring at the stars, waking up to a man who cared about my comfort more than his.

All of my moments with Ben are pushed to the back of my mind as Jason takes center stage.

Instinctively, my hand twitches, as if feeling the ghost of his touch, but his hand is no longer in mine.

This thought pulls back to reality enough for me to lift my gaze back to the man at the end of hall, his hand—the hand I memorized the touch of—holding someone else's.

Swallowing the lump in my throat and gripping the strap of my purse, I escape the suddenly cramped hallway of Violet Hotel. My thigh starts to sting from the memories coursing through me.

Jason never left me. We never even dated. But my mind seems to find conjuring him in Ben's place funny.

I try to shake my head and force all of the thoughts to vanish, but they all reappear front and center in my mind until I'm left with the memory of Jason rejecting me at the hospital.

We spent a month together. We danced, hugged, nearly kissed. He wiped my tears and gave me a nickname after a goddess warrior.

What's even worse: he told me countless times that he doesn't feel the same and we can't ever amount to anything. Yet, my heart hasn't learned its lesson because it's holding onto the bars of its prison, hoping with the little fire left inside it that Jason will—

Someone's hand gently wraps around my wrist, but the contact sends enough of an electric current through my veins for me to spin around and face the very man of my thoughts.

This close, his face looks different than it did days ago. There's no sun to highlight the creases and very faint freckles on his face. His dark hair isn't windblown but combed to perfection. He's not in those tan scrubs he wore all the time, despite the rest of his team wearing casual clothing, but in a suit that fits him entirely too well.

And, the most crucial and heart racing detail of all, his chocolate eyes are melting with the same longing I'm sure is reflected in mine.

No.

I'm wrong, again, because his hand lets go of my wrist and he takes a step back. "Sorry, I…"

There's a strong desire to keep my gaze glued to the floor, but doing so will only make it seem like I still have feelings for him and not some silly crush like I'm sure he thought it was.

So I straighten my spine, despite how much my limbs shake, and offer a small smile. Then, I do what I do best: act. "Funny seeing you here. I didn't expect you to be much of a fancy party type."

He studies me for a moment. "I'm not. It's actually my…" He rubs at the back of his neck as if the words are too painful to escape him.

Is it this hard to be around me?

Ignoring the ache in my chest, I change the subject to save him from having to give any personal details up to me. "You clean up nice, though."

"Thanks."

There's an awkward pause between us. The first since the day we met. I never thought I'd feel so uncomfortable around him with how much *he* calms me.

As I stand here, it's as if an ocean is between us and the fire he usually lights inside me has been swept up by a wave.

"Camila, I—" he starts at the same time, I say, "I should go."

His hand dangles between us like he meant to reach for me but decided better of it. Depositing his stray hand in one of his pockets, he nods. "Right."

"It was nice seeing you, Doc." I start to back up, hoping the distance will soothe the ache in my chest, but each step only seems to make the organ in my chest even weaker. "Have fun at your party."

Before he has time to answer or respond, I spin on my heel and book it out of the hotel. It's only when I'm outside and a drop lands on my crossed arms that I realize I'm crying.

They aren't horrible sobs like with Ben and there is no stairwell to hide in.

Instead, silent tears pour down my cheeks as a handful of people pass by me.

I wipe them away, swallowing the lump in my throat, as I hail a cab. Only when I'm in the back seat and on the way back to my apartment do the tears start to fall too fast for me to keep up with making them disappear.

CHAPTER THIRTY-THREE

JASON

"Camila, wait!" I shout as I sprint out of the hotel.

Out of all the places to be on a Friday night, she's *here*. At the Violet Hotel. At the same place and time I'm supposed to announce my engagement.

The second I saw her in the hallway, the past month flashed in my mind like a montage of all of my dreams changing and shifting with her involved in each one.

I couldn't move fast enough to excuse myself from Jasmine and chase after her. I only got as far as stopping her in the lobby before I froze up again.

What do you say to the woman you are madly in love with when you are supposed to be announcing your engagement to another woman?

> **Dilemma:** a situation in which a difficult choice has to be made.
> **Predicament:** a difficult, unpleasant, or embarrassing situation.

My heart broke into pieces the second her nickname for me fell from her lips. Then, she wore the fakest smile I never knew a person could own. But she did. She boarded herself up with armor because I made her believe I'm someone she needs to guard herself against.

I froze and let her walk away again.

But not this time. This time, I'm going to catch her before—

I come to a stop on the sidewalk outside the entrance, heaving in gulps of air as I watch Camila speed away in a cab.

For the fifth time in less than two weeks, I've made another decision to add to the long list of regrets.

"Hey," Jasmine places a hand on my shoulder as she appears beside me. I try not to stiffen under her touch, but I'm too numb from watching Camila walk away *again.* "I fully expected you to run away and hide in the shadows during this party like you tend to, but can you at least wait until after we make our appearance."

When I meet her gaze, her expression so amused and familiar, my chest seems to split even more.

I'm such an ass.

I wanted this. I wanted a family, and I forced Jasmine at my side.

Running away to chase after another woman is not what I should be doing.

Plastering on a smile and shifting so her hand casually falls from my shoulder, I offer her my elbow. "Sorry. Needed some air."

She continues to joke, and I laugh and groan at all the right parts as we make our grand entrance into the room as an engaged couple.

"What do you think?" Jasmine spreads her arms out to gesture at the connecting living room and kitchen as we move out of the foyer of the house.

After a painstakingly long night at our engagement party, she decided to show me the house she bought for us. My hope is that walking through it will remind me of why I proposed all those months ago.

The walls are not painted the dull white, gray, and black we're both used to. Instead, the floors are hardwood and there's color everywhere. It's not bright splashes of paint, but it's pale yellows and browns and greens as if nature crept its way inside.

My gaze snags on a painting of purple lilacs hung on the wall above the couch. The same design on Camila's dress when we went to the beach.

Then, as if that reminder of her was all it took, she starts to appear everywhere I look.

Jasmine gracefully sits on the brown sofa, but I see Camila curled into a ball as she sleeps, just like she was on the plane. Except in this situation, she's in my house and I could wrap a blanket around her to keep her warm. Or cozy in behind her.

When Jasmine shows me the kitchen, it's not her I see at any of the spots inside.

Instead, I see a woman with short black hair dancing at the stove in the way she danced at the refuge, except this time she's in my kitchen with my hoodie on instead of her brother's. I watch her flick her gaze over her shoulder and give me the biggest grin.

I see Camila sitting at the dining table with a little girl who shares the same crooked smile as Camila sitting right next to her.

Jasmine leads me up the stairs and in and out of the many bedrooms. She's talking to me. Painting our future life in front of me, but it's not her I see anywhere in this house.

I want to say that maybe it's the house that's the problem and we should find a new one, but deep down I know it's not.

Because I don't just see Camila here. I saw her in the car and walking on the street and in every corner of my mind. Worse: I *feel* the loss of her.

I can't escape her, but I'm not sure I ever really tried.

My heart aches in my chest as I watch Jasmine spin around in our master bathroom with the biggest grin on her face. "Is this what you envisioned for a family home?"

"Jaz…"

She must sense the sad tone wrapped around my words because her arms drop back to her sides. "You hate it. Well, it's too late to—"

"It's not the house. I…I don't think we should get married."

"Aren't I the one who is supposed to be getting cold feet? I already have penciled it for about five minutes before walking down the aisle." She pretends to check the pale orange watch on her wrist. "So you're going to have to hold off until—"

"This isn't just cold feet, Jasmine."

This seems to be enough for recognition to set in because she nods absently, her gaze not meeting mine, before she sits on the edge of the bathtub, gripping the sides of it.

Jasmine doesn't break down. Not with witnesses. Even now, if I didn't know her so well, I'd say she just got tired of standing and decided to sit.

But the issue is I know Jasmine like the back of my hand. It's one of the reasons I asked her to marry me to begin with.

"I'll call the caterer tomorrow," She starts to list her tasks off as she pulls her phone out of the pocket of her pale pink sweatpants and types. "And I'll cancel the band and send a note to the florist. Oh, your mother has the guest list. Do you think she'd be able to call—you know, what? I'll just swing by and—"

"Jaz, why aren't you mad or upset about this?" I come to sit across from her on the floor, my back against the wall.

She looks up from the phone. "Am I supposed to be?"

I scoff. "Considering you've planned everything to a T and been nothing but the perfect fiancé only for me to get off a plane and cancel the whole thing? Yeah. You should be pissed."

"It does blow that I have to tell your mother and my father that we aren't getting married. Oh, and my sisters. God, they'll have a field day with this."

She sits the phone down on the ledge of the tub beside her and stretches her legs, crossing them at her ankles.

"And I wish you would have admitted this *before* we announced our engagement to the world, but it's better late than never, I guess."

"Jasmine," I try again.

She releases a long breath. "You're not the only one who's been having doubts, Jay."

I stay quiet, waiting for her to elaborate because something tells me my doubts aren't the same as hers.

"I want a family. That hasn't changed, but…being here," she waves her hand around the space, "and preparing this house…it made me realize that I don't just want someone to live in it with me. I want someone to *build* it with me. To make it ours."

Her words aren't meant as an insult and I don't take them as one.

"So I don't blame you for wanting to call it quits. I'm actually relieved you did. Although, it would have been nice if you did this yesterday because I already talked to my landlord about my lease."

"I'll pay the extra it costs to get your place back."

"How about you talk to the parents instead?"

This makes me laugh. "Deal."

We settle into a quiet moment of understanding between us as the tension in my muscles releases. Suddenly, I realize I never gave her my reason and while she didn't ask and I don't usually give information unprompted, I blurt it out anyway.

"I met someone."

The corner of her mouth lifts in a smirk as she crosses her arms. "I know I'm probably supposed to get mad at you and accuse you of cheating and all of that."

"But?"

"That's it. Just that."

If I had a pillow, I'd throw it at her.

"Who is she?"

It's the first question I have been asked in a long time that makes me break out in the biggest grin. I tell her everything about Camila as if I am an artist talking about his muse.

CHAPTER THIRTY- FOUR

CAMILA

I rarely drink, if ever. I have found that the taste of beer and most wines does not fit my taste buds, and there's very few mixed drinks I actually enjoy. My alcohol preference is not the reason I find myself inside *Last Call,* a bar.

Lily invited me out to meet Piper and Hazel, her new friends. Although, something tells me she's more so using Hazel for her baked goods, but I can't say I blame her. I'm still floating on cloud nine after eating that croissant a week ago. It was a great way to get back to society.

"You're going to love them," Lily says as she guides me inside and to one of the booths in the back. "They always know how to have fun."

"Didn't you just meet them?"

"Yeah."

She stops us outside of a booth where two women sit. One has auburn red hair, freckles along her face, and golden-green eyes. The other, despite her curly brown hair and brown eyes, glows with yellow from the dress she's wearing to the bow in her hair.

She likes yellow. Noted.

"You're here!" Yellow exclaims and instantly I know why her and Lily get along so well. They're both eccentric. "I'm Hazel," she clarifies as I slide into the booth beside Piper—I assume—and Lily slides in beside Hazel. "And this is Piper."

"It's nice to meet you," Piper greets me softly with a small smile.

I nod, smiling back. "I'm Camila."

"We know," Hazel says. "Lily has told us so much about you. Well, in between her writing and your brother."

I half-scoff, half-laugh. "Yeah, they're not the biggest fans of each other."

At this, Hazel and Piper share a look before Hazel comments, "That's not the vibe I got."

Lily rolls her eyes and does what she does best: deflect. But I tuck that information away for later. *She* has *always been a sucker for an enemies to lovers romance…*

We fall in and out of conversations, mostly consisting of Pier and Hazel speaking in some weird code half the time—I guess that comes with such long friendship—and Lily's out of the ordinary comments.

It's different from what I'm used to, being here with the three of them. I'm not the social one between Lily and me. It's hard to even talk and be around Lily sometimes, let alone other people. Especially over the past few years.

But now, sitting in this booth around people who laugh and smile and joke with another, it's like taking a hot bath after a long day of work. It's relaxing and rejuvenating and exactly what I need.

So I dive into the conversation too, forgetting the mask I usually wear and just *living*.

"I can't believe you did that," Lily says through a laugh to Hazel.

Piper just told a story of Hazel running out in front of a car to save a bag of her cookies. Apparently, bakers have no sense of danger.

"I wasn't going to just let them get crushed," Hazel notes. "Besides, it worked out since the driver happened to be *quite* the driver, if you know what I mean."

At this, we all laugh.

Piper, after swallowing a gulp of her water, fixes Hazel with a stare. "Wasn't the driver *Oliver*?"

As if Lily is a dog that heard the word treats, she leans closer. "Who's Oliver?"

Hazel rolls her eyes, waving a hand in dismissal, but it's Piper who answers. "Her boss and secret crush."

"The owner of the restaurant."

"Yes," Hazel gives Piper a pointed look. "Emphasis on *boss*."

Lily squeals with excitement. "This could be the start of a fantastic romance." She takes a sip of her daiquiri.

"It would be with any other two people as the characters. Oliver and I are just friends."

"He seems to think otherwise," Piper adds.

"Please, I irritate him on a daily. He nearly had a cow this morning because I accidentally lost his place mats. Honestly, I'm surprised he hasn't fired me yet."

Piper, Lily, and I all share a look with one another, reading between the lines that Hazel can't seem to do. After a minute, the three of us burst into laughter before someone interrupts us.

"Hello everyone," a sophisticated voice comes from beside me. I look to my left to find a tall woman dressed in a pencil skirt and teal blouse standing beside her with her long, dark hair falling over her shoulder in a braid.

Something about her seems familiar, but I can't place it for the life of me.

"Jaz," Hazel greets back. "We haven't seen you in forever. It's almost like you're planning a wedding or something."

Without an invitation, Jaz grabs a chair from a separate table and slides it up to the edge of our table between Lily and me. "You thought planning a wedding was a headache? Try canceling one."

"What happened?" Piper asks.

Jaz opens her mouth to respond when her gaze lands on me and Lily and something must click inside. "I'm sorry. I didn't even introduce myself. I'm Jasmine. A friend of Graham's and Jason's."

That name makes my stomach flip. *It's not him.*

"Camila," I say at the same time Lily introduces herself too.

"Now that everyone knows everyone," Hazel interrupts, "Can you please elaborate on this wedding canceling."

Again, Jasmine opens her mouth to answer when someone else comes up to the table, stealing the breath from my lungs.

"Hey," he starts, but stops the second he sees me. His eyes go wide and he stands frozen to the spot like he's seeing a ghost.

My body seems to do the opposite though as my heart picks up speed like it's galloping in my chest. Suddenly the room is hot and humid. There's a strong urge to start fanning myself, but it might cause too much attention.

He isn't supposed to be here. We had a truce and I promised to stay away from him. I promised to keep my feelings at bay because he's clearly not interested and yet, here I am. *We* are.

Sweat starts to lick at my hands, so I reach for my glass in hopes of the cold drink helping to chill the heat inside me, but I misjudge the distance, and my glass knocks over the second my hand makes contact, causing the drink to spill over the table and down the side onto my lap.

"Shit," I curse aloud as I instinctively scoot back further against the seat to escape the beverage.

A rush of hands reach for napkins and start to sop up the mess. Everything is fuzzy and blurry around me, and I can't think straight enough to help.

I grab a napkin and try to clean up the sticky mess all over me when a cloth appears in front of my eyes. "Here."

When I glance up, Jason's chocolatey eyes are staring down at me.

That gallop my heart was doing a minute ago? Now it's come to a halt, trying to catch its breath as it stands on the sidelines, watching Jason.

I'm not supposed to like him.

"It's fine," I say as I push out of the booth, not taking his offering, and head straight for the bathroom.

My only hope is that he's gone when I get back or I come up with a good enough excuse to leave.

CHAPTER THIRTY-FIVE

JASON

She's here. The woman who's been stuck in my mind since the day I found her on the side of the road. The woman I called off my wedding for. The woman I never thought I'd see again.

Yet, here she is, sitting at the same table as the three women who have consumed my life.

Camila Martinez. Bellona.

I'm frozen in place, watching her as I'm tempted to pinch myself and test if this is real or not. It must be a figment of my imagination because everyone seems to be carrying on like the world hasn't flipped upside down.

Hazel mutters something about being interrupted again, but I'm too hyper focused to hear her properly.

I open my mouth to say something, anything, when Camila reaches for her drink and it spills. The brown, red liquid coats the table and drips off the edge onto Camila's legs. It lands a little on Jasmine too, but I'm too focused by the curse that escapes Camila's mouth.

As if my body is finally catching up with my brain, I walk to the bar and grab the rag off Graham's shoulder.

"Hey!" He calls after me, but I ignore him.

There's only one goal I have in this moment and it has nothing to do with the questions I'm sure he's going to lay out.

When I'm back at the table, I hold the rag out to Camila—the other four women at the table audibly surprised I'm not offering it to Jasmine. "Here."

She glances up at me, finally meeting my gaze head on, and my knees nearly buckle beneath me.

For the past few weeks, I've been beating myself up about the fact that I can't be with her and I have no way of contacting her. Now, here she is, and I'm single, and the only thing I can manage to say is, "here."

God, I'm an idiot.

Idiot: a stupid person.

Fool: a person who acts unwisely.

"It's fine," she says before swatting my hand away, standing, and walking away.

I stand, frozen in her wake, the cloth still in my grasp. It's only when I feel it disappear that I snap back to reality.

"Hope you don't mind if I use this instead?" Jasmine asks as she starts to dab at the liquid that fell on her legs.

I rub at the back of my neck.

"Do you know her?"

How do you tell your ex-fiancé that the woman you broke up for and who has been rampaging your mind is the same woman who just spilled her drink everywhere?

"That's…Camila."

She stops dabbing and looks up at me. "*The* Camila? The one from the refuge?"

After we decided to end things, I gave Jasmine a run down of just about everything that happened this past month. She wouldn't have let me give one-word answers anyway if I decided not to.

Then, I repeated it all to Graham when I got home later that night. Both looked me square in the face and asked, "How are you going to get her back?"

As I stand here and stare at the spot she vanished from, I find myself asking that same question. And just like when they asked me, I have no fucking clue.

"I'm sorry—" Hazel cuts in. "Someone clue me in on what is going on."

Piper must have kicked her underneath the table because Hazel sucks in breath after giving Piper a pointed look.

"*Please.*"

"Oh my God!" the woman with blonde hair sitting beside Hazel—who I only just realized is here—holds a hand over her mouth as she stares wide eyed at me. "You're him."

"Him who?"

"You have some nerve coming over here after the way you treated her." The woman crosses her arms.

"What did you do to her?" Jasmine asks.

I'm getting whiplash just from trying to keep up with all of these women now staring at me and waiting for an explanation. One I'm not sure how to give.

"I—" I start, but another person interrupts, patting a hand on my back as they say, "Why wasn't I invited to the party?"

"I have never been so frustrated in my entire life," Hazel exaggerates in her corner. Piper scoots Hazel's drink closer to her, a silent reassurance.

"Why is everyone staring at me like predatory owls?" Graham asks as he removes his hand from my back.

Jasmine stands, grabs a chair from a separate table and pulls it up beside her. "Sit." She tells both me and Graham.

Graham slides into the booth beside Piper, mumbling about how there is a mound of napkins on the table, while I take the chair by Jasmine.

"Why do I feel like I'm in trouble?" he attempts to whisper to Piper before wrapping an arm around her shoulders.

"You're not the one who's in trouble," Piper answers as she tucks further into his side.

"Start talking," the woman who has yet to introduce herself to me demands.

Everyone's eyes fall to me. Some with the most accusatory looks and others with genuine curiosity.

I glance in the direction of the bathroom Camila ran off to what feels like forever ago, but she's still nowhere in sight.

Releasing a sigh, I tell them everything. "Camila and I met at the refuge a month ago."

Maybe not everything because that's where I stop. What else am I supposed to say? Give them the entire play by play of the past month?

Not only does that require more talking than I'm a fan of, but there is one person at this table that I'd rather not know certain things, and a person who has yet to introduce herself.

Although, she apparently knows at least some semblance of what happened because she's the first to say. "Seriously? That's all you can say? You led her on for weeks, only to turn her down the second she told you she liked you."

"Who are you?" I ask, but it gets interrupted and ignored.

"You led her on?" Jasmine asks. "You didn't tell me that part."

"You knew?" Hazel looks to Jasmine.

"Of course I knew. I'm his ex-fiancé."

"We still haven't heard that story yet."

"Jay and I ended things when he got back."

Everyone stares between us, then at each other. God, my head is pounding from all of this.

Graham and Jasmine already know the full story so why they are not helping at all is beyond me.

I kick Graham's ankle with my foot and grit out, "Help me here."

He holds his hands up in mock defense. "Hey, don't pull me down with you. I'm as clueless as they are."

The women ignore him, knowing full well how much a liar he is, before they each start to grill me again.

I open my mouth to tell them to stop talking, but the woman of discussion returns to the table before I have a chance.

She stops hesitantly between Jasmine and I—an irony that isn't lost to me—and flicks her eyes at everyone, but me. In fact, with how much she's avoiding looking at me, you'd think I'm not even here to begin with.

"I think I'm going to head out," she points a thumb over her shoulder.

My heart sinks to the pit of my stomach. Out of everyone here, the one person I don't want to leave is the same person who can't get out of here faster.

The group is freakishly quiet as we all sit with bated breath, waiting. For what, I'm not sure.

When Camila reaches for her purse she left sitting on the table and makes a motion to leave, I grab her wrist without thinking.

She stares down at my hand, not meeting my gaze. For the first time, her touch doesn't calm me, but sends enough electric through me to make me feel like a live wire.

"Don't leave," I request.

I squeeze her wrist once to say "Please."

Twice to say, "Not yet."

A shuddering breath escapes her before she finally looks me in the eye with the tightest smile I've ever seen. My heart stops beating in my chest and my blood turns cold.

Truce: an agreement between enemies or opponents to stop fighting for a certain time.

She called a truce between us, but...

Enemies: a person who is actively opposed or hostile to someone.

An enemy wouldn't make feel as alive as she does.

Hostile: marked by malevolence.

Her touches are as gentle as a feather falling to the ground.

Hostile: openly opposed or resisting.

This, this definition seems to be the most honest one in this moment.

She's not resisting me. She's resisting the feelings she has for *me* because I asked her to. Because I *told* her to.

When she adjusts the strap of her bag on her shoulder, realization and hopelessness settles into me like the hardest pill I've ever had to swallow.

Despite how much I missed the warmth of her touch and how much everything in me is screaming to not let go, I do. And just like that, she's out the door with the blonde haired woman hot on her heels.

CHAPTER THIRTY-SIX

JASON

"Don't tell me that after all of that, you're just going to give up," Hazel says as she sips from her third drink of the night. "You can't just sit here and wallow when there's someone as madly in love with you as Camila is."

My heart is too tired from the whirlwind of today to laugh or deny her claim. "She won't even look at me." I've messed up everything.

"Because she's in love with you and you haven't so much as smiled at her!" Hazel says the words like I'm the most impossible human being alive.

Honestly, I just might be.

"I think what Hazel's trying to get at," Piper adds softly from across me, "is that you have a chance still. If you like her…you should go for it."

After Camila and Lily left, the remaining five of us gathered around the table as they all grilled me for every single piece of information. When I laid my heart bare for the third time in the past week, they started asking how I'm going to get her back.

The same question Jasmine and Graham asked me separately. The same problem I have yet to find a solution to.

"What do you want me to do?" I ask as the irritation starts to return. I'm utterly hopeless and out of control and it's driving me crazy. "I don't have her number to call her up. I don't have her address to show up at her door and talk to her. So what would you guys have me do?"

"You aren't thinking logically," Jasmine leans back against the booth seat where she sits beside Hazel. "If you call her or show up at her door, she might find it more creepy than romantic."

"I think it's romantic," Graham adds. "Just show up with one of those singing groups who will sing a love song to her."

Piper taps his chest and shakes her head, a silent warning to stop talking. I've never been more grateful about the two of them dating.

"Or," Hazel starts, "you do something smaller, but equally important."

"Like what?"

"What means the most to her?"

I straighten in my seat as I pick at the beer in my hand. The conversation I had with Camila about her ex floats back to me. She never said it aloud, but I know she secretly just wanted someone who's not scared, but proud to have her next to them.

This, though, isn't something I can tell the four sets of eyes peering at me. It's not my secret to share.

"Why?" is all I offer.

"Because, my romantically challenged friend, it's your ticket in. The key to any lasting relationship: trust. So, show her you listen to her too and you're not going to make the same mistakes any other guy would."

She's right and it's a great idea. *If* I had the means of contacting her that is.

As if reading my mind, Jasmine pulls out her phone and says, "Add her on social media first."

"That's a great idea!" Hazel copies Jasmine, pulling up Camila's Facebook profile.

Apparently, Hazel met Lily—the woman with blonde hair and Camila's best friend according to Hazel—a few weeks ago at work. They hit it off, something that comes so naturally to Hazel, and the rest is history. Lily met Piper and Graham through Hazel. All three of them met Camila earlier tonight.

And I happened to stumble into the bar at just the right time. Although, none of it seemed to be what I needed it to be.

"Here it is," Jasmine shows me her phone and beckons for mine.

I'm not a big social media person, but if this gets me in contact with Camila…

Jasmine taps away at my screen and when she's done, she announces, "Voila! Now you just have to wait for her to add you back."

Suddenly, all of my newfound hope disappears. "What if she doesn't?"

"She will."

"Here," Hazel starts tapping away on her phone. "I'm texting Lily for her address."

"Didn't you all just say that's creepy?"

"I didn't," Graham notes from his spot.

Usually, he'd be more involved in a conversation like this. Or any conversation for that matter. When Piper's around, though, she seems to settle him. Instead of the buzzing bee he tends to be, he becomes a tame cat lying in the sun when he's in her presence.

"You," Hazel tells him, "Are not a reliable advisor."

"I got Piper, didn't I?"

"You got Piper because she's blind and can love you past your faults."

Piper nods in agreeance and coos, "I do love you."

"I love you too, Trumpet." He kisses her forehead.

Hazel groans at their display of affection, but there's a small grin she's holding back. Hazel is a romance fiend. Especially when it comes to the people she cares about.

Normally, I'd groan and ask them to be anywhere else when they are this affectionate, but all my brain seems to conjure is Camila and I in their place.

God, I've got it bad.

"Oh, Lily answered," Hazel interrupts my thoughts. "And because I'm such a likeable person, I've got Camila's address. Just sent it to you."

My phone pings on the table, but I don't make a move to grab it. "You all want me to show up outside of her door without a warning? That's one of the worst ideas you've ever come up with."

"I'm going to try and not take offense to that, especially when you are in such dire need of our help. But to answer your question: no. You aren't going to show up at her door unannounced. You're going to send her flowers with a card. Make it sound as less creepy as possible."

Flowers with a card. The only issue is I don't know what kind of flowers are—

Lilacs. Purple lilacs.

They were on her dress the day we went to the beach. It's both a memory of us and a sentiment to her.

I pick up my phone and search for a florist nearby. It's too late to call any, but I can set a reminder with their information in it for tomorrow morning.

It's not a perfect idea and she may never open up to me again after I shot her down, but I have to try.

After spending most of my life tense and looking for the next thing to tell me I'm doing everything right, she came along. Her gentle caresses were nothing but a storm of energy and light inside me.

I can't give that up without a fight.

CHAPTER THIRTY-SEVEN

CAMILA

Most people hate the rain. It's cloudy, gloomy, wet, and gross when it rains. I understand where they're coming from, but it'd be a lie to say I feel the same.

The rain has always been a calming shower on my runs and makes me push myself harder. So here I am, wearing a pair of spandex shorts and an oversized t-shirt as I run down the sidewalk back to my apartment.

A few of the passing pedestrians give me second glances, but I ignore each of them as they rush by in suits and sweats and heels and just about every type of outfit one could imagine.

I round the corner, and my apartment building appears before me. It's not the best place with the withering exterior and cracked walls, but it's an affordable roof over my head.

My apartment is only a few stories up with two apartments on each floor, so I jog up the steps, my sneakers squeaking against the floor from the rain.

I'm covered in a mixture of sweat and rain and probably smell worse than when Paxton made salmon for the first time. A steaming bath with the scent of lavender and some upbeat music fills my mind. There's nothing more enticing after a run in the rain than a sh—

I come to a slow halt outside of my door, trying to catch my breath, as I stare at a vase of purple lilacs sitting on my faded welcome mat.

What the hell?

Paxton never sends me flowers, nor does Lily. My parents wouldn't either. Even if they did, none of them know my favorite flowers are lilacs.

So who…?

I bend down to pick up the vase and a letter appears beneath it. Picking it up too, I unlock my door and carry both inside.

There's no thought to kick my shoes off or take a shower before I set the vase down on the coffee table and rip open the letter.

It's not in an envelope but is folded three times with a piece of tape on the outer edge. Unraveling it, I pray that it isn't from Ben. As soon as that thought crosses my mind, I laugh aloud.

Ben would never do such a thing.

When the letter is open in front of me and I start to read the typed---not written---words, the laughter dies.

Bellona,

> *There is an upcoming charity gala and I remember you saying how much you've always wanted to experience a black-tie event. It's at the time and location below.*

> *You're welcome to bring Lily or anyone else you want with you. There are two invitations tucked in here.*

Jason.

Jason sent me my favorite flowers.

Jason invited me to a charity gala.

Jason—

Wait. How did he get my address? And why is he inviting *me*—the same woman he turned down less than a week ago—to a charity gala?

Although, the two tickets I'm now holding in my hand make me wonder if this is just because of the other night. An olive branch because after I called a truce, I left the bar the second he showed up all because I'm too weak to keep my feelings at bay around him.

I run, don't even say hi, and he sends me my favorite flowers and invites me to a black-tie event.

He added me on Facebook that same night too and I ignored it. Actually, I threw my phone and nearly rolled off the couch from how surprised I was.

My phone rings on the counter, interrupting my thoughts. "Paxton's Work" rolls across the screen and for the first time, I hesitate in picking up my brother's call.

He didn't handle it very well when I told him Jason rejected me. Paxton likes to joke and make things light, but that switch flips instantly the second someone he cares about feels down.

Biting my lip, I watch it ring and ring until I finally come to the conclusion that I can answer without saying anything about the flowers or the gala.

I pick up the phone and swipe to answer it before pressing it to my ear. "Hey, Pax," I singsong as I maneuver towards the bathroom to the bathroom to get the shower started.

"What did you do?" he accuses.

My heart rate picks up. "What makes you think I did something?"

I imagine he's squinting his eyes and leaning arm on the wall like he does when he catches someone in a lie. "I don't know." He uses a high-pitched tone. "Maybe it has something to do with how high your voice is."

Steam starts to fill the small bathroom as I weigh my options. Lie or lie? Lying seems like the most viable option right now.

"Camila Briar Martinez."

"Hey, what are you middle naming me for?" It's easier to come off defensive when he annoys me.

"Well, maybe if you tell me the truth, I wouldn't have to."

I swipe a hand at the mirror to see my reflection once again. I'm blurry in the mirror with my hair framing my face in a sweaty, humid mess. My cheeks are flushed pink but it's not from the run.

There were times during and more times after Ben that I stood in front of this very mirror and stared at myself for hours. I would grab a sharpie and outline the flaws on my skin. I'd try on a thousand different outfits and get rid of any that made me look like a sack of potatoes or showed the worst parts of me like my big arms from lifting weights, or my thick thighs.

Elizabeth was thin and perfect. I'm muscular and stout.

I'd compare myself endlessly and obsess over every difference between us until I finally comprised a list of a hundred-fifty-three reasons I could understand Ben chose her over me.

That list was shredded and burned over a week ago.

Now as I look in the mirror, all I see is a work in progress. Not in the way that I have so many flaws and could never be a runway model pretty, but in an on my way to loving myself type.

I'm far from perfect and I never will be, but that's not what I care about anymore. I don't need someone to choose me when I've spent so long choosing others over myself.

It's time *I* pick *me*.

So I turn off the shower and go back out to the kitchen as I tell Paxton, "I'm going to a charity gala."

"A char—did you get rich and not tell me?" he asks.

"Why would I tell you if I got rich overnight? You'd be the last person I tell."

"Oh, come on. I'd tell you if I won the lottery."

I pick up the vase and put it on the coffee table instead where the sunlight hits, breathing in the scent of the lilacs. "You wouldn't have it long enough to tell me about it."

He scoffs. "You can't just let that kind of wealth collect dust, Camelot."

I laugh as we continue to go back and forth. When we're done, I hang up and jam out in the shower as I imagine what gown I will be wearing this weekend.

CHAPTER THIRTY-EIGHT

CAMILA

"Remind me to visit your brother sometime," Lily whispers beside me as we walk inside one of the ballrooms—from the size and luxury of it there's no other way to describe it—of the Violet Hotel.

After I showered and changed, I called Lily and told her about the flowers and about the tickets. Her response was "If you tell me you aren't going, I will kill off Zach in the next chapter."

I laughed. "I don't think that's the threat you think it is."

"How do you feel about this…?" she asked slowly. "The whole Jason sending you flowers and inviting you to a gala thing, I mean."

My fingers skimmed the letter sitting on the coffee table. *Bellona*, he addressed it with. He remembered my favorite flowers. He remembered a story I told him. And, even after how I treated him and threw myself at him, he called me Bellona.

"I want to go," I told Lily, and it felt more honest than I've been in years. "And I want you to go with."

Every part of me wished the letter said he wanted me to go as a plus one, not for me to bring a plus one. But this was just something nice he's doing for me. A friendly act of the truce.

It's not a date.

"Aren't you and my brother in hate with each other?" I ask Lily in the present as we saunter through the room.

"You know what they say: keep your friends close and your enemies closer. Plus, if he's got friends like this…maybe I'm enemies with the wrong people."

I chuckle and shake my head.

The room is filled with perfectly positioned black standing tables around an elegant dance floor in front of a stage with classical music playing. A few couples are dancing slowly to the music and my gaze catches on a specific pair.

A certain ruby red haired woman in a green dress in the arms of a man with shaggy blonde hair. Piper laughs as she nuzzles into Graham's chest. His face is beaming with happiness like he's perfectly content swaying with her in his arms.

My chest squeezes at the sight, but it's not from the same green monster that used to attack me. Instead, I smile at the two of them.

"You have to try these," Lily shoves a layered cracker in my face. It looks like there's a sliced olive, cheese, and some kind of meat on top of this professionally baked cracker.

It feels too fancy to devour the way Lily is, but I take it anyway. When I take a bite, it becomes an impossible task to swallow.

"I thought you said this tastes good," I mumble through the bite at Lily.

She grins as she shows me the rolled-up napkin in her hand. "If I had to experience it, you do too."

"You're evil," I joke.

Lily simply shrugs as we stand off to the side and observe the party. Surprisingly, we both managed to scrounge up some gowns in time for this event. Lily has more connections around the city than someone in the mafia. She found us something affordable and stunning.

Well, I panicked about my dress all up until we got in the car and I had no way of changing out of it.

Lily picked a slim, baby blue dress with thin straps. After only trying on one other dress, she insisted I wear the purple gown I'm wearing now.

The torso is snug around the chest and waist with off the shoulder sleeves. The rest fades into a semi poofy bottom with a leg slit. The material is slick and smooth between my fingers.

I'm scanning the room when a flute of champagne appears in front of me.

"Is this another attempt to get me to try something disgusting?" I ask, not taking it.

"What was the first thing I convinced you to try?" a familiarly rough voice, one that does not belong to Lily, has me freezing.

I glance at the man to the right of me, ignoring Lily's snickers beside me, and am met with a pair of melting brown eyes, like the chocolate chips of a gooey cookie.

He's dressed in a suit with a black bow tie at his collar, similar to the other night in the hallway. I've only ever seen him in casual clothes and scrubs and if I found him attractive then…

My mouth becomes dry, and I realize it's hung agape as I stare at him.

Flicking my gaze away, I grab the flute from his hand and chug a much bigger gulp than is probably appropriate. It fizzes on the way down, nearly making me gag.

God, this is embarrassing.

Instead of disappearing like I expect and pray for him to do, he settles beside me, clasping his hands behind his back. He doesn't say a word, just stays calm and quiet.

Does he not feel as off kilter as I do?

Obviously not because I'm the only one with a heart beating out of their chest.

Stop it, I demand myself.

I sneak a glance at him out of the corner of my eye with the champagne glass coasting along my lips.

He buys me flowers, invites me to a gala, and then just *stands* there.

Suddenly, enough annoyance fills me for me to mumble, "You invite me just to avoid me?"

"I'm not avoiding you," he's quick to respond.

"Seriously? You haven't even looked at me at once."

Not that I expected you to.

Something grazes my right hand by my side and look down to find his fingers dancing like a ghost along my knuckles. If he feels the electric shock from the touch, he doesn't make it noticeable.

"I haven't been able to take my eyes off you since the moment you walked through the door, Bellona."

His admission steals my breath and has me dropping the glass to my side so I can peer up at him better. When I do, his gaze is already locked on me.

"I've been trying to not throw myself at you. That's why I'm standing here like an idiot."

He can't possibly mean what I think he means, can he? *No.* He made it perfectly clear he's not interested, but God, does my heart wish he did.

I turn away from him and take another sip of the bubbly drink. "Thank you for inviting me. This is a nice event."

He moves and offers me his arm. "Want me to show you the best part?"

I stare at his arm, waiting for an explanation. He simply motions to the dance floor with his chin and the softest smile on his lips.

"You want to dance?" I whisper as if someone will hear us.

"If you'll let me."

With a hesitant nod, I place my hand on his arm and he guides us to the center of the room. At some point during this conversation, Lily wandered off. I had been so surprised by Jason that I didn't even realize she left. Although, considering she gave him my address, something tells me she was up to this.

When we're on the dance floor, Jason situates us so one of his hands is on my back, one of mine is on his shoulder, and our other hands are interlocked beside us. Slowly, he guides me to the music.

I haven't danced since that day at the refuge with Jason. But that wasn't as intimate as this one feels.

I follow his steps carefully, watching our feet, until he asks, "Have you never danced before?"

Peeking up at me, "Do nightclubs count?" It's the same thing I said at the refuge and just like then, it makes him smile and shake his head.

"Do people dance like this in night clubs?"

"No. It usually consists of more grinding and bouncing than this."

He leans in so his mouth is pressed against my ear, making all the hair on the back of my neck stand on end. "Am I disappointing you?"

I inhale a scent of his shampoo as I whisper, "You're confusing me, Doc."

He pulls back to meet my gaze, but I duck my head before he has a chance. I'm not ready to face his rejection again. Not when his arms make me feel so content and warm and safe.

I'm not ready to give that up yet.

He doesn't seem to hear my pleas though because he says, "I need to be honest with you, Camila."

"Don't. I got it. You aren't interested in me." I try to pull out of his embrace, but he only yanks me tighter.

"Why do you keep saying that?" There's a crease between his eyebrows.

I ignore the itch in my fingers to smooth it out. "Because you've said it about a hundred times now."

"No. I didn't." His fingers graze between my shoulder blades in the lightest touch. "I said that I couldn't date you, but I never said I wasn't interested in you."

"What are you saying?"

"I want to be completely honest with you, Bellona. Not just because that's what you deserve, but because I want this—us—to go somewhere. I don't want to keep doing this back and forth and I never want to hear the word 'truce' come from your mouth again. So I'm going to tell you something and I need you to hear me out from start to finish."

I swallow the lump in my throat as I give him a short nod. My palms are sweating, and I want to pull away before he notices, but he won't let me. He squeezes my hand twice in his as if to say, "thank you."

"Before I left for the volunteer work, I proposed to a friend of mine. I think you met her for the briefest moment the other—"

"Jasmine," I fill in the blank as that night refocuses in my mind.

The woman at the end of the table dressed in a professional outfit with her long hair and flawless skin. She didn't introduce herself, but started talking about how her—

"Oh my—you're her fiancé."

All of the times Jason told me he shouldn't be hugging me, holding me, shouldn't even be near me...

They hit me like a blow to the gut.

I pull from his hold, but his grip tightens slightly.

"Let me go," I grit out.

"Before you start panicking," Jason interrupts my thought, "please just let me explain."

"You're *engaged.* You didn't think to mention any of this during the *month* we spent time with each other."

"I know. I should have told you. I'm sorry."

I don't know what else to say. Every comprehendible sentence seems to be out of reach. I try to piece everything together, but it's all one big mess.

So I let him start to sway us again. When I don't say anything, he continues.

"I've always wanted a family of my own. Now that I'm getting closer to thirty, I thought I should settle down. And who better to do that with than the woman my parents have pinned me with since the day I was born? I knew she would be a good mother to my children and, while we aren't in love with each other, we would be respectful to each other."

I let his words sink in, wondering what on Earth he's doing dancing with me and not trying to win her back instead.

"She felt the same, so we put together a contract and decided to marry when I came back. But…"

He squeezes my hand once and uses his other hand to guide me closer to him, a silent request for me to look at him. I do and the warmth in his gaze erases all doubt from my mind as a fire lights inside me.

"Then I met you," his words are breathless as they coat across my lips from his proximity.

Kiss me, I internally whisper.

"And now I have a new wish. I don't want to sign my life away for something safe and mediocre. I want to be with someone who's stubborn even with a snake bite on her leg."

The memory of when we met flashes to me and a blush creeps onto my skin.

"I want someone who will call me out for being an ass instead of being scared to push my buttons. I want someone who dances like no one's watching and who will hold my hand even when I annoy the hell out of her. I want to be with someone who makes me feel so unbelievably alive that I can't remember what life was like before her because now all I see is her."

If my heart was running a thousand miles a minute earlier, it's sprinting at an inhumane speed now. It pounds in my ears as my skin tingles from Jason's touch.

My gaze flicks to his mouth and I watch the way his lips carry his next words.

"I know I haven't been clear about my emotions, but I needed to end things before I pursued you. I didn't want to do to you what your ex did to you. And I didn't tell you any of this because a part of me hoped that I would be able to forget you and move on, but after only a month, you've carved yourself into my heart, Bellona."

"Jason…"

His eyes fall to my mouth, and I make that wish again.

Kiss me.

If either of us were to lean even a hair closer to the other, if we were to tilt our heads an inch…

I pull back slightly to gain even the slightest hint of clarity to think. "I don't understand."

Jason releases a sigh and rests his forehead against mine.

"I mean, I understand, but…you gave up a secure future for one with *me*? I can't promise you those things,

Jason, and I don't want to be the reason you are disappointed in the future."

I can't handle another guy walking out.

"I want those things with you." He lifts one hand to cup the side of my face, letting his thumb graze my cheekbone. "And I can't promise you that there won't be times you infuriate me. I promise that you will."

My fist lightly beats against his chest, which earns me a chuckle.

"I thought safety was something I needed, but after you…I want to be my own stunt double in this."

"That is the worst pun I've ever heard," I mumble with a grin on my lips.

"Did I at least work enough to convince you to go on a date with me?" His thumb moves down to graze my lips as his eyes study the movement.

"I'm scared," I admit for the first time in my life, but his touch sends a shot of courage through me.

He doesn't say anything. Just continues to caress my skin and wait for me to finish my thought. It's my turn to open up, I guess.

"I spent the past few years thinking about what Ben did to me and comparing him to every guy. I can't forget what happened. It's not that easy."

Every part of me has been trying to erase everything that happened. I hid all of the stuff that reminded me of him and spent countless hours at the dojo or curled up on the couch in hope of distracting myself long enough to forget.

But the memories won't leave.

As Jason's arms hold me tight in the warmest and most comforting embrace I've ever been gifted, I realize that it's not about forgetting.

I will never forget what Ben did to me or all of the sweet moments we had before that. They are memories I need to hold onto as both warnings and endearing moments to look back on.

"Trusting you is going to be hard," I tell Jason. "There may be times when I doubt even the smallest things. And I snap easily, and I hate being tucked in the shadows."

He pulls back slightly to meet my gaze. Placing both of his hands on either side of my face and grazing my skin with his thumbs. I move my arms, so they are around his waist instead of his neck.

We're both holding onto each other, needing space to say the things we feel, but not willing to let go.

"If you can handle that," I choke out, "and you're one hundred percent sure that you aren't going to change your mind about walking down the aisle tomorrow, then I want to try."

He tilts my head up with his fingers under my chin and shifts closer but stops when his lips are a breath from mine. My eyes fall close, waiting, hoping.

"Let me kiss you," he whispers. "Please."

I don't give him an answer. Instead, I push up on my toes and plant my lips against his in the gentlest press.

He freezes for a fraction of a second, surprised, before his hand leaves mine to cup my jaw. I wrap my arms around his neck in a silent plea for him to pull me closer.

Jason's teeth nip at my bottom lip as he pulls me flush against him as if he can't get enough of me. Although, I'd probably kill him if he let go.

When we finally pull apart to catch our breath, he nuzzles his head into the crook of my neck as I bury my head in his chest, suddenly aware of all the people around us.

"We just kissed in front of a room of people," I mumble.

He wraps his arms around my waist, tilts my head back up to plant a smiling kiss against my lips, and promises, "I will never hide you in the dark, Bellona."

EPILOGUE

JASON

THREE WEEKS LATER

When Camila opens the door to her apartment, she only peels it back a crack, barely letting me peek inside around her. The only thing I'm here for is the woman in front of me though.

It's been a few weeks since the night at the gala and is our first official date. We've been talking on the phone and meeting at the bar here and there, but neither of us have had a long enough span of time between my shifts at the hospital and her shoots for a new movie she's part of. Until today, that is.

"What's that?" A bandaged finger points at the flower in my hand.

I had the intention of buying her an entire bouquet, but the flower shop was closed today due to a "sudden illness" as the sign said, and everything was gone at the grocery store by the time I arrived.

Luckily, I was able to stop one of the customers before they left and paid him for one of the flowers from his bouquet. He wouldn't give up the whole thing.

"I believe it's a lilac." I twirl the stem in my hand. "If you open the door a hair more, you might be able to see it better."

She bites her lip, wagering on the idea. Suddenly, a sour feeling gnaws at my stomach.

"Is everything okay?"

"Promise you won't say anything?" is all she offers me.

"Like what?"

"Those comments of yours."

With an arched brow, and not knowing what she's referring to, I nod.

Slowly she disappears behind the door, then opens it completely, with her standing anxiously in the doorway.

She's wearing a white sundress with purple lilacs, like the one in my hand, dancing around the fabric. It hugs her chest in a modest way while having a slight poof at the end. My eyes get caught on the skin showing from a few inches before her knees all the way down the heels on her feet.

"I think this is worse than having you laugh."

My gaze snaps back up to her face. Her arms are crossed in mock defense, but I can tell she's nervous. She should never be nervous around me.

I take a gentle step closer, reaching my hand out to toy with hers. "Why would I laugh?"

She fiddles with the length of the dress. "I don't dress up like this often."

I'm within a foot of her, begging her to look up at me. "You wore a dress the day we went to the beach and at the gala."

"No, but that was different. A gala…you're supposed to dress elegantly. A date…"

One of my hands gently brushes her hair behind her ear, then cups the side of her face, finally gaining her attention. "You look beautiful, Bellona."

The nickname sends a pink blush to her cheeks, and I fight the grin filling my own features.

It would be so easy to lean in and kiss her. To finally have my lips crash against hers in a gentle swarm of warmth and understanding of just how breathtaking she is.

Since we kissed that night, I've been craving to do it again like it's my next breath.

Before I have a chance, she steps out of my touch, grabs her purse, and motions to the door. "Ready to go?"

I regain my composure, clearing my throat. "One second." Taking a step closer, I tear the stem of the flower, then tuck the bud behind one of her ears. When I finish and step away…

Breathtaking.

The pottery class is a short walk from Camila's apartment. I considered driving, but that wouldn't allow me to truly be beside her. I crave to be near her like she is the air I breathe.

I peek down at her as we walk. Her hands are wrapped around my arm. I've only ever held hands with a girl, but after having Camila's thumb trace smoothing circles on my skin, I only ever want this. Holding hands does not compare to this kind of intimacy.

But I only ever want *Camila's* hands wrapped around me.

"Is this it?" Camila asks.

I look at the building beside us. "Pottery" Is inscribed on the bricks above the doors.

I open the door for her, ushering her inside. When we step in, there are a variety of creations littered on the floor and shelves around us. From generic bowls to oddly shaped decorations, there are hundreds of clay sculptures.

The only light is from the sun peeking through the large windows on the right wall next to the door. It illuminates a few of the glazed pieces and creates a rainbow-like image on the wall.

"Jason," Mr. Farkle comes through a beaded curtain from the back, heading straight towards me.

He attempts to give me a hug, but I'm quick to shake his hand instead.

It doesn't deter him, though, instead he laughs and addresses Camila while pointing at me. "This one never lets anyone get ten feet of him. I'm not sure he'd even let you poke him with a stick."

My chest tightens and my fists clench at my side. He's not making me look good like he promised. Then, I hear a small laugh escape from Camila and all of the tension seems to dissipate.

I run a hand through my hair as embarrassment flushes my skin from her amused stare.

"Well, sweetlings," Mr. Farkle holds his hands out beside him as if he were offering us something. "The studio is yours for the hour. Just be sure not to touch any of the existing creations. I will be in the back if you need me."

With that, he walks back through the curtain, just like I paid him to. Moreso promised to pay for his next medicine refill, but all that matters is he's giving this space to us.

"This isn't a class?" Camila asks me from her spot.

A blush creeps up my skin as I rub at the back of my neck. I told her I signed up for a pottery class. I didn't tell her that it would just be the two of us.

Rolling up my sleeves, I reach for the aprons hanging on the wall behind a few wheeling stations. "No. It will just be me and you."

"But we don't know how to make pottery."

"I never said I didn't know how." I pass her one of the aprons before looping my own around my neck, then tying it around my back.

She sets her purse down and starts to do the same. "You know how to work with clay?"

I shrug. "How hard can it be?"

She starts to scoff, then stops and raises a brow at me. "Wait. You didn't bring me here for one of those *Ghost* reenactments, did you?"

Yes. Yes, I did. "I have no idea what voodoo stuff you are referring to." Yes, I do, but she clearly does not like that idea so that will be thrown out the window.

When I finish tying my apron, I see she is still struggling with hers. Cautiously, I come behind her and stop her hands with mine, taking the strings from her.

"Let me."

Her breath hitches, but she removes her hands and lets me tie the apron for her. I take my time as I let my fingers occasionally brush against her.

If I can't hold her while we do this, I can at least find an excuse to touch her.

It's tied, but I stay still for a minute, soaking in the moment before she pushes me away. We may be dating now, but I don't want to push her or make her think I'm only with her for her body.

The last thing I want is to make her feel the same way her ex did.

"Is it tied?" She reaches behind her again, her fingers nearly brushing mine.

My chest pounds with my erratic heartbeat at her closeness. I clear my throat. "Yes." Quickly, before I do something rash, I move back to the wheel.

She sits at the wheel beside me while I explain the basics that Mr. Farkle explained to me.

Then, we slap some clay on the wheel and start molding our own creations. We're lost in the motions, or at least she is. I'm pretending to shape something, but my eyes keep drifting to her. Loving the way she bites her lip as she concentrates on the task.

Her fingers are covered in the mud and I realize the apron may not be wide enough to keep her dress from getting splattered.

I turn my wheel off, stand, grab another apron, and bring it to her. Gently, I lay it across her lap. It's only then that I notice she kicked her shoes off. I nearly laugh at the sight.

"What are you doing?" Her wheel is turned off and she's staring down at my crouched position.

Her heart is thumping frantically, or is that mine? Something is beating so loud it's hard to think straight. My fingers are burning with electricity and that's when I remember I still have my hands on her lap. Quickly, I pull away and stand.

Not cool, Jason. Not cool.

"Sorry," I run a hand through my hair, but it gets stuck in the tendrils, reminding me of the clay in my hands. "Shit. I—"

She's laughing. A full-blown belly laugh that makes all of the embarrassment go away. I would gladly embarrass myself if only it would elicit another laugh from her. If only it will permanently make the skin around her eyes crinkle in amusement.

I lied earlier. *Now,* she is breathtaking.

She stands and goes to the sink. After cleaning her hands, she waves me over. "Come here."

I do so without hesitation, and I realize I would do anything so long as she's the one who asks.

She wets her hands again, then reaches up to comb her fingers through my hair.

Her touch drives me wild, and I nearly groan from the contact. She has to stand on her tiptoes to reach so I bend my head down a little, making sure not to touch her with the clay still on my hands.

"It's not going to be perfect," she tells me. "But it will at least be clean enough until you shower later."

I see the words escaping her lips, but I'm too focused on the lipstick coating them and wondering how her lips would feel against mine to understand her properly.

Her fingers continue to comb through my hair. She dives back into the water for a quick second, but when she focuses back on me, she freezes. She must see the desperation and longing in my eyes because I swear I can feel her breathing slow.

Her heart has to be beating at the same erratic pace as mine. There's no way this is all in my head.

I wish my hands weren't covered in gunk and she wasn't clad in a dress she cherishes because every fiber of my being is begging me to reach out and touch her.

Just one caress. Just one.

But I know that if I do, I won't be able to stop. So I swallow every emotion and tear my eyes from hers. "Is it clean?"

She shakes her head slightly before reaching her dripping hands back up to comb through the strands once more. "There."

Camila doesn't look at me when she removes her hands from me. Just wipes them on her apron and moves back to her station.

Suddenly, the air seems to shift and I wonder if I did something wrong. Did I do something wrong? Did I offend her? Was my hair greasy?

"Thank you," I whisper to her as I come to sit beside her.

"Mhmm," is all she says without glancing up at me.

When I sit back down in my seat, far too quickly does she lean over and plant a kiss on my cheek. I barely have time to register before she's back in her seat.

"Did you just…?" I start, at a loss for words.

There's a smile she's fighting as she says, "Your clay is going to dry if you keep wasting time."

Before I can overthink, I lean over, tilting my head to press a soft kiss on her lips. A gasp escapes her, and I grin as I settle back in my seat.

She starts to chuckle softly beside me and shakes her head with amusement. It makes my chest warm with love because that's what this is to me. Love.

I am madly in love with Camila Briar Martinez, my personal Bellona.

Love: an intense feeling of deep affection.

One day, I will tell her that too, but for now, I resume making the vase I intend to gift her with. After I fill it with lilacs, of course

TOUCH DATES

A COLLECTION INSPIRED BY CAMILA & JASON

- Cuddling under the stars
- Tango dancing
- Sparring (preferably in a non-threatening way)
- Building clay sculptures (but definitely not reenacting that scene in Ghost)
- Dancing at a gala
- Taking a walk (while holding hands)
- Play a game of Twister
- Picking flowers

Camila & Jason's Touch Playlist

A GUIDE TO HEALING

- Hugging:
    - Helps to boost mood
    - Good for the heart
    - Calming
- Holding hands:
    - Decreases stress
    - Creates a level of intimacy
- Small touches:
    - Lowers heart rate
    - Decreases depression and anxiety
    - Relieves pain (in some cases)
- Kissing:
    - Melts tension
    - Decreases stress
    - Burns calories
    - Shows love
    - Encourages emotional bonding

ACKNOWLEDGEMENTS

Book two is officially on the shelves and off my desk (which is of course an exaggeration because I still have printed copies of two drafts on my shelves and five drafts in my computer)!

This book took a handful of rewrites and finding the perfect rhythm between Jason and Camila. They are two people who shy away from touch but are drawn towards one another without a clear explanation as to why. Their story, like all of the others I have written, is close to my heart and I'm so delighted to share it with the world.

I'd like to say thank you to Summer, my ridiculously supportive best friend who read three drafts of this book, ran through idea after idea with me, and gave me brutal honesty even when I didn't want to hear it. You are a saint, Summer, and a big part of as to why the book has become what it is today.

Mckenna, my sister and one of my closest friends, thank you for taking time out of your already jammed packed schedule to read this story and boost its writing. I appreciate everything you do and you have no idea how much of a help you are!

Next, I'd like to say thanks to the people who have passed in and out during my writing spurts, or been present during the phase of ripping the story apart for edits. If it weren't for you, I may not have ever gotten off the couch and eaten more than a cereal bar.

Thank you to everyone who has inspired this story and boosted my creative flow enough for this book to make it to the shelves.

Lastly, to every reader that has opened this book and read. Whether you lasted the entire book or only made it a few words, I appreciate you giving it your consideration. Camila and Jason's story is close to my heart, and I hope you will be able to find some comfort in this book just like I did.

Thank you!

ABOUT THE AUTHOR

Chloe Riggs is the author of *Soulmates are Overrated, Falling for the Sound of You, Reviving From the Touch of You* and many short stories. *Soulmates are Overrated* is her first published book, but she is prone to have a handful of drafts on her desk waiting for the finishing touch. She is known for writing fictional romance with gut-wrenching emotions.

She was born and raised in a small town of West Virginia. She worked in real estate and travel writing, observing all types of people and gaining lots of inspiration.

Chloe has been writing since she was younger. The love for putting her imagination into words on a page has always been a talent of hers. She hopes to be able to share these wild stories with a wide audience that is just looking for a great escape from the stresses of reality. You can find more of her works at blooming-narratives.com.